The Best of
Frontier Tales

Volume 4

Visit our website at
www.Pen-L.com

ISBN: 978-1-942428-35-0

Cover art: *Cowboys in the Bad Lands* by Thomas Eakins, 1888

Interior and cover design by Kimberly Pennell

The Best of Frontier Tales

Volume 4

2012–2013

Winning short stories from

FrontierTales.com

$\mathcal{P}$

Pen-L Publishing

Fayetteville, Arkansas

Pen-L.com

Dedicated to those who love the creak of saddle leather, a dance hall piano, and the smell of horse sweat and gun smoke. Saddle up for some fun times!

From the publisher

These stories are as they come from the authors. Some of them may have small errors. All writers need an editor and a proofreader. However, Frontier Tales is a "for the love" project and there are insufficient time and resources to supply professional services. So if you find an error, just bear in mind that we try our best to provide something for everyone who loves Westerns . . . even the nitpickers! ☺

If you'd like to take a gander at our other Frontier Tales anthologies of winners, hopalong to **www.Pen-L.com/Westerns.php**. You'll find lots of other good books at **www.Pen-L.com/Books.php** too. Thanks for supporting your Western authors!

The Tales

Lowell "Zeke" Ziemann

Zeke's love of the Old West began in the '40s and '50s watching the "Oaters."

He earned a Master's Degree in Mathematics and coached and taught for sixteen years. His athletic and coaching skills earned him induction into three Halls of Fame. He entered the financial services industry, eventually serving as the Compliance Supervisor for the Arizona office of a Wall Street firm.

He semi-retired in 2007 and began writing Western short stories, some of which received high praise and rewards. His stories have been published online, and four anthologies and two novellas are available on Amazon.

His diligent historical research of the Old West and his vast library become apparent as his stories accurately reflect the settings, language, and conditions of the time.

He can be contacted at: zekeziemann@reagan.com

Doc's Warning: "Play Poker!"

by Lowell "Zeke" Ziemann

"Whoa," yelled the driver as he reined in the four horse hitch. "Welcome to The Flat at Fort Griffin."

Twenty-three-year-old John Henry Holliday stepped down from the stage coach. Always conscious of his appearance, John used a glove as a duster and applied it in brisk fashion to his hat. He swept his tailored grey suit, and used his hanky to wipe the dust from his boots.

At the Planter's Hotel he rented a room, opened his valise and hung up his clothes. Carefully, he laid his medical case on the dresser, opened it, and found all of his instruments had survived the trip without damage. He left the room, locked the door and walked out to the street to look over the town.

On the mesa that rose above the town, the Stars and Stripes fluttered over Fort Griffin. Below the fort, on a broad, dry plain, stood the commercial site nicknamed "The Flat" by its thousand or so inhabitants. Canvas tents, framed stores with false fronts, and drab, tawny adobe huts lined the single thoroughfare. Next to the sheriff's office, carpenters were building a small jail. There must be a dozen saloons, he thought.

Bored soldiers from the fort, bedraggled buffalo hunters returning from the Great Plains, and lonely cowboys driving herds to the railhead at Dodge City shopped for supplies and milled around on the boardwalks that paralleled the sides of the rutted street.

Commerce flourished. Merchants supplied an abundance of vital goods and services. Saloons provided lusty, twenty-four hour recreation.

Of course, when settlements like The Flat boomed, the gamblers, card sharks, prostitutes and drifters always followed.

John Holliday's stoic youthful face suddenly broke into a slight smirk. There's opportunity here, he thought. Whether he practiced dentistry, or gambled, John could smell money floating around.

He stopped at the fanciest looking joint in town, the Bee Hive Saloon and walked in. He went to the end of the bar.

A well-muscled bartender was telling a ribald joke to a tall, rather stiff looking man with a silver star pinned on his dark vest.

The barkeep wore a long white apron. He approached and stuck out a meaty right hand. "John Shanssey, owner, operator. What'll you have stranger?"

"Whiskey," said Holliday as he laid a coin on the bar. "Ah'm John Henry Holliday. Just came in on the stage."

"John Holliday? I heard of you. You're Doc Holliday, the gentleman dentist and gambler."

"Ah've been called worse," said Doc as he shook the big man's hand. The husky bartender laughed.

Doc noticed an empty Faro table standing adjacent to the bar. He paused for a second or two and searched the face of John Shanssey. The pug nose and a cauliflower ear marked him as a pugilist. The big Irishman smiled and his eyes twinkled with friendliness. This man can be trusted, he thought.

"Ah would appreciate an opportunity to deal Faro here in your saloon."

"I know you've had experience dealin' Faro and I could use a dealer . . . if there shan't be no trouble."

"Ah dealt in Dennison and Dallas. Made big profits both places. If ya'll care to stake me occasionally in a poker game, ah'll include that also. Ah'll pay the house twenty five percent of the take. Those, sir, are mah terms."

Shanssey nodded. "Twenty-five is fine."

"Ah'm obliged. Ah'll start tomorrow afternoon after ah hang out my dentist shingle at the hotel. Ah'll practice dentistry mornings."

Doc threw down the jigger of whiskey, and Shannsey poured another. "On me."

Doc scanned the saloon. Four cowboys played poker at a table in the middle of the room. Then his sweeping gaze stopped abruptly and he focused on the raven-haired beauty sitting alone in a corner booth. He nodded and touched the brim of his hat. The curvaceous woman bowed her head slightly and returned a smile. She wore little powder or paint. This woman is not just another soiled dove, he thought.

Her long dark hair and flawless, glowing face reminded Doc of Mattie, the love he'd lost back in Georgia. First distanced from her when he'd headed west to relieve his diseased lungs, then any hope for the relationship brought to a close when Mattie entered a convent. Once again he fought off the lingering pains of loneliness, homesickness, and the dark fate of consumption. The memories haunted him, and surfaced all too often.

"John, introduce me to that woman."

Shanssey took Doc over to the table. "Kate, this is Doc Holliday, my new Faro dealer. He just arrived in town."

The woman looked up from her Solitaire game. She glanced at Doc's clean and pressed suit, and studied his face. Her devilish green eyes seemed to stare right through him. Daintily she extended her hand. "Kate Elder, my pleasure."

Doc kept holding her hand as he sat down. He studied her creamy complexion as he sipped the jigger of whiskey. "Y'all work here?"

Kate snuffed out the cigarette she held. "Yes, but not as you think. I only cater to the occasional well-to-do clientele." She cocked her head to the side. "Why do they call you Doc? Are you a doctor?"

"A dentist, and . . . a sporting man."

"My father was a doctor." Her eyes seemed to sadden. "He died when I turned sixteen. I quit my studies and hit the road. Been traveling ever since."

Doc sat back, smiled tenderly, took a tobacco pouch from his vest pocket and rolled them each a quirley. He handed one of the smokes to Kate and sighed. "Miss Kate Elder, you're a helluva fine looking woman."

ft

Shanssey backed away from Doc and Kate and returned to his friend who leaned on the bar studying Holliday and the woman.

"Guess it's love at first sight," said the man with the badge.

Shannsey laughed. "Kate is her own woman. She'll decide if it is love."

The tall lawman moved close to Shanssey and whispered. "So that's Doc Holliday huh? He's a killer ain't he?"

"Well Wyatt, he ain't killed nobody hereabouts. He's gonna dentist and run my Faro table. Stick around awhile and I'll introduce you."

Wyatt Earp straightened his vest and turned to go. "Later John, I'll be in tomorrow afternoon. I'd like to meet him before I go. I'm headed back to Dodge City in a couple more days."

ft

"Ho-oh," yelled Ed Bailey.

The wagons stopped. He checked the three flat bed racks loaded with buffalo hides and re-fastened a couple of loose tie-downs.

Circling the entire train, he inspected the mule's harnesses, the wagon tongues and the greased wheels before he climbed back into the lead wagon and signaled the drivers to continue. It was only seven more hot and dusty miles to Fort Griffin and every hide was precious. He and his crew shot and skinned buffalo on the Great Plains for the past three weeks. The hunt had been hugely successful. Now was the time to deliver the goods, pay off the boys, gamble, and spend his earnings on wine, women and song—though he didn't intend to sing much.

The wagons carefully crossed Clear Creek, near its junction with the Brazos River. The pungent odor of a gigantic pile of drying buffalo hides stacked at the edge of town reached Bailey before he saw them.

"Whoa, whoa there mules," Bailey shouted as they entered The Flat. The wagons creaked to a stop.

He got down and approached the small office that stood on a muddy corner at the edge of town. A short bow-legged man, dressed in an ill-fitting suit and carrying a worn green ledger stepped out to meet him. "Quite a load you got there Ed."

The little man eyed the three racks. "Here's my offer. The goin' price ain't but five dollars per hide."

"Jules, you better sharpen your pencil. Try seven," said Ed as he attempted to scratch some of the grime off of his beard.

Jules leaned forward and cupped his right ear. "Eh?"

Bailey took a step toward the buyer. "Jules, ya damn old four-flusher, yer not hagglin' with no greenhorn here. Don't ever try to bulldoze me agin, or we might have a blow-up."

Jules retreated one step, then stopped and rose up on his tiptoes. "Bailey, yer a bull headed, hard old polecat. Six-fifty, and no more," he said with his voice rising.

"Done," said Ed with a satisfied chuckle. "Pay me in cash, and soon! Five boys throwed in with me and are hankerin' to get their wages and raise a little hell."

Jules went to his shack and returned with a fist full of greenbacks. Ed gathered his crew. "Here you go men. Each man's pay plus a ten dollar bonus." The men hoorayed. They grabbed their money and headed for the saloons, dancehalls, or the alley cribs.

Bailey stuffed the balance of the cash into his pocket and walked to the hotel. He reached his room and hung up his buckskin coat. After pouring water into the basin, he took the soap and tried to wash three weeks of stench from buffalo guts and hides off of his hands and arms. He donned his one spare shirt, slicked back his greasy hair, and stuck his six-gun in his coat pocket. A good poker game is what he needed. "I'll be damned if some tinhorn gambler is gonna fleece me this time," he said out loud to himself.

f_t

Ten days after arriving at Fort Griffin, Doc looked over the hotel room he had adapted into a dental office. A roll top desk held the medical case that contained his instruments. A rocking chair that could bend backwards would be used for patients. He perched on a tall three legged stool to do the work.

Doc had pulled a rotten tooth out of the mouth of an old trail boss that morning. He folded his pay of three dollars, placed it into his pocket and moved to the rocker to relax.

Doc was tired. Most mornings he filled or pulled the tobacco stained teeth of cowboys or smelly buffalo hunters. Afternoons and nights were spent in the Bee Hive dealing Faro or playing poker. Both activities required acute concentration. Sleep was disrupted by occasional coughing fits followed by medicinal jiggers of whiskey. The strain left him exhausted.

Doc's mind wandered over the acquaintances made since coming to town. His reputation usually caused strangers to regard him with suspicion, fear, or utter disdain. That's good. It kept adversaries wary, unwilling to mount a challenge. But Earp is an unusual lawman. He displayed only curiosity and accepted Doc without judgment. Cold and calculating, no ruffian will get the bulge on Wyatt Earp. He's nearly like family, he thought.

"Ah need a friend . . . and one like that," Doc said to himself. "Wyatt wants me to go to Dodge City . . . might do it too, when this town plays out."

Doc shook his head and smiled. "And Kate, beautiful and charming Kate. Would she go with me to Dodge? Hot blooded woman, yet with a soft heart. Nice to have occasional conversations with an educated lady for a change. But damn, she can be regular hell on wheels when riled. Never a dull minute with Kate. What a daisy, a real daisy."

f_t

Kate rolled out of bed. She had shared his life for nearly two weeks now. Doc's deep throated cough commenced as he woke up. A short jigger of whiskey from the bottle that stood on the nightstand quelled the raspy hacking. He set the glass down, sat up and slowly began to dress. Doc's gold watch, lying next to the bottle, indicated that it was nearly noon.

Kate dressed in the rose-colored frock that Doc purchased for her a day earlier. While he dressed she primped in front of the standing full length mirror. She wanted to look good for him. Furthermore, she cheerfully provided a foxy distraction for card players who ogled her as she stood behind Doc during poker games. Picking up the small matching purse she asked, "Where will we go for breakfast?"

Doc stepped in front of her and placed his silver stickpin in the middle of his black ascot. He admired his grey suit and powder blue shirt, donned his Prince Albert coat and grabbed a towel to dust off his boots. Now fully awake, a smug, confident look adorned his pale face. "Let's go to Shansseys' Bee Hive and have the café send something over. There'll be a game there this afternoon. Some buffalo hunters came in last night. They'll be full of drink and backed up with plenty of cash."

f̧t

When Doc and Kate pushed open the swinging doors of the Bee Hive, John Shanssey rushed to meet them. He nodded toward a corner table. "See those four playin' stud over there? That black bearded galoot is Ed Bailey. He's a rough customer, and he'll hornswoggle you if he can. Best watch him close."

Doc grinned and Shannsey continued. "The old trooper sittin' next to Sheriff Jacobs comes in here whenever he's off-duty. His name is Dugan. He's a straight shooter. The young drover I never saw before."

Then he slipped Doc forty dollars, winked and spoke in a low tone. "Bailey brought in hides yesterday. He's flush."

Doc walked to the table. Kate followed. Ed Bailey looked up. "Care to sit in?"

"I'm your huckleberry," said Doc. He nodded to the sheriff and took a seat to the left of Bailey. Kate moved close behind Doc.

Wide-eyed, the young cowboy's mouth dropped open as he stared at Kate. The soldier slowly stroked his flowing mustache and gazed at her with covetous eyes. With a coy smile, Kate adjusted the neckline of her low-cut dress.

Bailey paid no attention to Kate. He counted the stack of bills in front of him. Three members of his crew, however, stood at the bar and watched her every move.

Kate noticed Sheriff Jacobs fix narrowed eyes on John Henry Holliday. A slight frown grew on the lawman's face. There had been no trouble in The Flat, but apparently exaggerated rumors of Doc's previous altercations with the law preceded him.

Doc's face lit up in a slight smile as he dealt the next hand. "Draw poker."

Kate knew the smile was part of the scheme. A confident smile when he dealt, when he looked at his hand, when he bet, and when he won. Even when he lost a hand the grin was there. It was Doc's poker gambit—meant to keep the other players guessing; and it worked.

Kate marveled at Doc's hands; small, clean and delicate. Whether used for dentistry, dealing cards, as a gunman, or as a lover, his hands operated proficiently. This man, she hoped, would take her out of this hellhole known as Fort Griffin.

Doc could laugh or curse with equal ease. He had few friends, but to those he trusted, he demonstrated loyalty to a fault. Drunk or sober, fearless and yet remorseful, sardonic and witty, despondent or sarcastic, Doc Holliday's moods were difficult to anticipate. Though unpredictable and possessed of a quick temper, Doc drew her like a moth to a flame. And whether he would admit it or not, she knew he needed her as well.

Consumption rendered Doc unable to defend himself in possible rough and tumble saloon brawls. Therefore, he always armed himself with a nickel plated .45 pistol carried in a shoulder holster, as well as a long dagger tucked into his breast coat pocket. Potential foes were convinced that he could be lethal with either.

After Doc dealt the five cards to each player, Sheriff Jacobs opened with a three-dollar bet. The trooper tossed in his cards, as did the young cowboy who continued to ogle Kate. Bailey called Jacobs' bet as did Doc. Jacobs drew three cards, Bailey one and Doc took two. They all tossed their waste cards into a pile. Brazenly, Bailey reached over and began to look at the discards.

Doc lowered his head, squinted through slits of eyes and pointed a finger at Bailey. "Ed Bailey, have you sir, no knowledge of poker rules or etiquette? Don't monkey with the deadwood! Play Poker! Peek at the discards again and you lose the hand!"

Bailey grunted, smirked, and growled a string of obscenities. "I play with my own rules."

Doc opened his coat and tapped the butt of the six-shooter in his shoulder holster. He spoke in a somber, but certain tone. "Ah advise you sir, not to monkey with the deadwood. Play poker."

Sheriff Jacobs diffused the tension. "Take it easy boys, let's have a friendly game." Then he looked at his draw and bet ten dollars. Bailey threw a defiant look at Doc and raised the bet ten more dollars. After Doc called, Jacobs folded his cards and got out.

"Two pair, aces and jacks," beamed Bailey.

"Three little fours. Ain't that a daisy," announced Doc. His grin returned and he drew in the pot.

"Damn!" growled Bailey. Several of Ed's friends gathered around the table like bodyguards.

Sheriff Jacobs dealt the next hand. After a round of betting, draws and a second round of betting, only Doc and Bailey were still in. Bailey again reached over and took a peek at the discards.

"You were warned." Said Doc as he casually folded his hand and began to draw in the pot.

Bailey jumped to his feet and shouted. "Damn you and damn yer rules." He rose and kicked out a leg of the table.

The table flipped over sending cards and drinks flying. The trooper, still seated, tipped over on his back . The cowboy kicked back his chair and hastily ran for the door.

Bailey reached in his coat pocket, came up with a pistol and threw down on Doc. Before he could cock the gun, a bright crimson stream of blood strained through his shirt and flowed steadily from his midsection. A deep gash ran from under his right ribcage to his left hip.

Ed's scream cut through the smoky saloon like a clap of thunder. "Eeaagh! Boys! Boys! I'm cut! I'm cut bad! I . . . I . . ."

Ed dropped his gun, grabbed his stomach and crumpled to the floor. One of his crew rushed to him and rolled him on his back. The bloody mess spread on the hardwood floor. Ed's associate wrinkled his nose, choked, drew back and put the back of his hand over his mouth. Ed Bailey suddenly lay quiet and breathed his last.

Sheriff Jacobs drew his gun. "The knife Doc, give me the knife . . . and your pistol."

Doc handed the weapons to the Sheriff. Blood from the long knife dripped on Kate's new gown. She took a step back.

Three of Bailey's crew slowly advanced. One of them yelled. "Get a rope!"

"Get back. I'll drop the first man who moves!" warned the Sheriff, pointing his six-shooter at the nearest buffalo hunter. "There'll be no lynching here. Doc, you're under arrest."

Kate looked at Doc. He seemed remarkably calm. A buffalo hunter stared at Doc with venomous eyes, a set jaw and veins that bugled from his neck. He turned his glare to the sheriff, but remained where he stood.

Kate's stomach tightened. Her hand shook as she reached into the small purse. Her fingers closed on a small derringer, but left it alone. "There's too many. Calm down," she told herself. "I gotta do something. Think, think."

Jacobs grabbed Doc's arm as he kept a steady eye on the crowd. They backed toward the door. "Stay put," the sheriff shouted. Upon reaching the entrance, the two men turned and quickly departed. Doc did not look back.

The friends of Bailey retreated to a far corner of the saloon and formed a tight circle. They talked quietly.

Trying to collect her composure, Kate hurried to Shannsey. "Help me John. We've gotta do something. Those buffalo men will find Jacobs and rush him. They're gonna hang Doc!"

Shannsey took Kate's arm as he watched Bailey's crew huddle. He whispered. "Jacobs will take him to the hotel. We'll have to get him out of there."

ft

Doc looked around the hotel room. With his drawn pistol, Sheriff Jacobs waved Doc to a chair in the corner of the room and locked the door. He sat on a chair opposite his captive. "I see it as self defense Doc, even though I figured havin' a man like you in town could cause trouble. I'll hold you here until my deputy gets the judge . . . might take a day. You can bet that those buffalo men'll try to lynch you."

"Ah'm obliged Sheriff," said Doc. "But I'm afraid if you don't get help quick, that'll be the end of John Henry Holliday."

Buffalo hunters were hard men, accustomed to handling life or death situations on the vast prairie. Some were killers. They escaped the law by disappearing on the Great Plains. After Bailey's crew made their plans they would be coming, and soon.

ft

With the plan set, calm and determination replaced panic. Kate looked to the big man she and Doc trusted.

"Are we agreed?" asked Shannsey.

Kate nodded.

"All right then, go to the big oak tree behind the wagon yard. It's in the willows down by Clear Creek. Give me about an hour."

Kate hurried to Doc's room at the Planter's Hotel and changed into a pair of Doc's riding pants and one of his shirts. She stuffed a pistol into her pants pocket. With an old hat pulled down over her eyes, she casually walked out of the back door of the hotel. She entered the barn out back and untied all of the horses. Picking up a pitchfork Kate threw some dry straw against the side wall, then opened the door and chased out the freed horses. A lighted match tossed into the straw immediately ignited a blaze.

Kate hurried to the front of the hotel. "Fire! Fire!" she shouted. She entered the hotel and continued to yell. Soon everyone within hearing distance was rushing, bucket in hand, to the blazing barn.

Kate returned to Doc's room and grabbed his medical case. Then she knocked on hotel room doors yelling "Fire! Fire!" Arriving at a room that was locked, she pulled the pistol from her pocket and pounded on the door. Sheriff Jacobs opened up to find the business end of a six-shooter thrust into his ribs. Kate pushed him with the six-gun. "Sit in the corner Jacobs."

Doc tied the Sheriff to the chair with a curtain pull. After he gagged him with his hanky, he and Kate hurried out of the room and locked the door.

ſt

As townsfolk rushed to form a bucket brigade to battle the blaze, the commotion, noise and confusion allowed Doc and Kate to scurry toward the willows behind the wagon yard. Two sturdy horses, already saddled, stood tied to a big oak tree. Rain slickers and a large bag of grub hung on the saddles.

Two weeks and four hundred miles later they rode into Dodge City. Doc signed the register at the Dodge House hotel as "Mr. and Mrs. John H. Holliday", and set up his dental office. His relationship with Kate and his friendship with Wyatt Earp were now cemented.

–The End–

Tim Tobin

Mr. Tobin holds a degree in mathematics from LaSalle University and is retired from L-3 Communications. He lives with his wife MaryAnn of thirty-four year and two cats in Voorhees, NJ. His two grandchildren, Maggie and Shawn are the joy of his life. Mr. Tobin continues his education by attending classes at Camden County College where he also volunteers his time. Eighty of his stories appear in print and online. Follow him on Twitter @TimTobin43.

The Buzzard's Tale

by Tim Tobin

The man lay face down in the gravel. The temperature in the noon day sun had risen to around ninety degrees but he was freezing. Blood loss, he knew, from being been shot, twice. Once in the arm and once in the leg. Neither wound would have been fatal if there had been anyone to help him, anyone at all. But he was alone and knew he was dying.

The man gave life one more chance. He crawled with his face in the dirt to a small rock. He pulled himself to a sitting position and then tried to stand. His left leg had a bullet hole in it and there was just no strength left in the right leg. He fell flat on his back. His eyes focused on movement in the sky.

Buzzards, a kettle of them, were circling, riding the thermals, smelling death coming. Their circular motion in the sky made him dizzy. Or was it blood loss? As he slipped into death he wondered why he was dying for a crime he did not commit. Where had justice been?

The buzzards swirled down to the ground. The large black male hopped towards the dead man and examined him closely. He flapped his huge wings and landed on a boulder where he watched the wake attack the corpse. What they didn't finish, the coyotes would.

ft

Infant Finn Becker and his family emigrated to the United States from Germany in 1825. His mother told him stories of survival in a big place called New York. Finn's father took a job on the waterfront and earned just enough to keep the family from starvation. Finn found a job alongside his father when he was ten.

He had no formal education but his mother taught him to read and write and how to do basic arithmetic. By sixteen he was hopelessly in love with Hanna Klein. In 1844, at the ages of nineteen and eighteen, Finn and Hanna married.

Lured by stories of opportunity in the West, the newlyweds packed their scant belongings. And with a few dollars in their pockets, they joined thousands of other new Americans in pursuit of a dream. They each took whatever jobs they could find to finance their slow trek west.

They had heard of a trail to a place called Santa Fe and made it their destination. As they slowly made their way west, two sons were born, William and John. Finn and Hanna made sure the boys had "American" names.

By 1850 the Becker family was on the Santa Fe Trail traveling west from Missouri in a covered wagon. Two months later they arrived in Santa Fe, in the virgin territory of New Mexico. The journey had been hard but there had been no Comanche or bandit attacks.

They surveyed the drab and dusty town and decided they had not yet found their dream.

They looked northward to the magnificent, towering Sangre de Cristo mountains. They looked south towards Mexico and found that sporadic war still raged. With no stomach or funds for travel to California, they decided on the mountains and drove their wagon north.

About fifty miles from Santa Fe they came upon a small village on the Santa Fe River named Broken Rock. Broken Rock got its name from thousands of large boulders formed by some long forgotten cataclysm. Broken Rock used the river for commerce, shipping lumber and firs south where they were bartered for essentials for the small village.

On their journey west, Finn had learned about horses and he and Hanna had talked about starting a small horse ranch. And here, near the riverbank and forest, they decided to build their ranch. There was water to drink and for livestock and wood for building a home.

Finn and Hanna built their first house by hand. They called it a cabin but it was really little more than a shack. But it was theirs. In the spring

Finn rounded up wild horses and then sold them to farmers, cowboys, soldiers, travelers, and explorers. By 1870 they were successful, if not rich.

The cabin long ago had given way to a log home with rooms for Finn and Hanna and the boys. They had a living room with a stone fireplace and a separate kitchen. A barn housed their personal horses and tack. A corral kept their wild horses until they were broken and sold.

Their sons, Willy and Jack, also grew, but they grew apart. Willy inherited his mother's physical traits. He was short, not topping five feet four inches. He was wiry and spry. Ranch work and defending himself when teased about his stature made him into a strong man for his size. Like most men of his time he wore a gun but not a low-slung, tied down Colt .45.

Rather he wore a small pistol in a holster worn on his pants belt. Many called his gun a ladies gun but it fit in his small hand just fine. He could shoot a snake if he had to and could kill a rabbit for dinner. He had never fired at a man and never wanted to.

Unlike Willy, Jack's physical attributes came from his father. He was tall and handsome. From an early age he learned that his size and looks could get him out of work. Jack would tease Willy about his stature and would bully his smaller brother into doing his chores. If Willy complained, he got beat up.

Jack didn't last beyond his sixteenth birthday on the ranch. His six-gun was low on his hip and strapped down. Jack was very good with his gun. His draw was quick and his aim sure. One day he just left. No goodbyes or see-you-laters.

And so Jack drifted the area surrounding Santa Fe and became a bandit, a horse thief, and a rustler. Occasionally he would stop by the ranch. Hanna would beg him to stay and Finn told him to move on. After taking money and supplies, he would always go. Willy was too small to stop his brother from stealing from his own family and Finn was always relieved when Jack left.

ft

Willy had driven a herd of mustangs into Santa Fe to sell at auction. After he concluded his business he deposited the proceeds at the bank, pocketed his pay and headed to the saloon for a beer. He was minding his own business when the Santa Fe Kid burst through the swinging doors, pushing men and working girls aside.

The new fellow wore two guns, butts forward like Wild Bill Hickok. The Kid was just plain mean and rumor had it that he had killed five men in gunfights. There had been many arguments about how fair those gunfights had been. He pounded the bar and demanded service. The other men at the bar gave way to his bluster.

Willy took a seat at a table and nursed his beer. The gunman bought a bottle and went to work. The whiskey hit him hard and fast. The Kid rose and pushed a few men out of his way. He stood at the bar and roared a challenge. "Somebody draw against me or I'll kill one of you just for fun." No one in the bar stood a chance but he paced around the bar looking for a victim.

His gazed settled on Willy and he yanked him to his feet.

"You'll do," he told Willy.

Willy was scared, more scared than he had ever been of his brother. The gunman pushed Willy into the street and told him to draw. Willy knew he couldn't win and turned away.

Jack rode into town as the gunfight was unfolding. He recognized the gunman and saw his brother was helpless. Jack wasn't helpless though. He had seen the other man shoot and knew he could take the Kid. But he didn't. He just chuckled to himself and wondered how Willy would get out of this.

The gunfighter drew his pistol and fired at Willy's feet. Willy froze. The gun on his hip was useless. The man fired again, this time a little closer. Willy fell to the ground in terror. The big man holstered his gun and Willy thought the danger might have passed.

Instead the man strode up to Willy and kicked him in the chest. And then he kicked him in the face. He picked Willy up by the shirt collar and beat him with his fists. He beat him until Willy was bleeding from his nose, mouth and eyes.

He probably would have killed Willy if the sheriff hadn't intervened.

He just ran the gunman out of town and a couple of deputies piled the pathetic Willy on his horse and slapped the horse on the butt. Instinctively the horse headed for home. All the while, Jack just looked on and did nothing.

Hanna was horrified at Willy's injuries. Broken Rock had no doctor so Hanna did her best to treat her son. Willy eventually recovered his health but not his pride. He was a broken man. Before the attack he had been fearful, helpless even; but now he was a coward.

His fellow ranch hands warned Willy that the Santa Fe Kid was looking for him. He wanted to finish the fight without the law interfering. Willy heard that the Kid was camped nearby. He would likely check the Becker ranch in the next few days. Willy didn't know what to do. He couldn't fight the man, and he couldn't run from him.

That night Jack rode up to his father's ranch looking for another hand-out. Willy went to Jack and begged him for help. But Jack just looked at Willy with contempt and told him to do his own dirty work.

Willy was terrified and alone. But a plan shaped up in his mind. With the family asleep and Jack in his old room, Willy snuck in and stole Jack's Colt and his boots. He crept out to the barn, saddled his horse and rode off as quietly as he could.

Willy had little trouble finding the Kid. He smelled the remnants of a camp fire and crept close enough for a look. Sure enough, his tormentor was there and asleep. Willy carefully removed his boots and pulled on Jack's boots. They were enormous on him but he didn't have far to walk. He cocked the Colt. The double click sounded like a shotgun going off but the Kid did not wake up.

Willy awkwardly covered the few yards to where the Kid was sleeping. He placed the gun between his shoulder blades and fired. The Kid pitched forward with an oomph. The Colt recoiled so hard that Willy dropped it in the dirt. But the man was not dead. He was struggling to reach his own pistols.

Willy desperately looked for the Colt. He finally found it and picked it up. The man was almost to his guns. Willy's eyes were wild with fear and revenge. He used both hands to cock the gun again. And this time he fired directly into the man's head. Blood and gore spewed everywhere; the Kid was definitely dead, shot twice from behind.

Willy sat on a rock and let his heart return to normal. When he stood up, he purposely walked in the dead man's blood.

He retraced his steps, changed back into his own boots and rode home. The ranch was quiet. No one had missed him. He snuck back into

Jack's room and replaced his gun in its holster and put his boots back by the bed. Willy went to bed and slept fitfully.

Willy wasn't very surprised the next morning when the sheriff and his deputies rode up to arrest him. Apparently someone had seen the dead man and reported it. And, as the sheriff pointed out, Willy had a motive.

"What kind of gun was used?" Willy asked. The sheriff shrugged.

"Hard to tell," he said. "Something large caliber."

Willy pointed to his holster and the small gun. The sheriff smelled the gun and checked the chamber. The small caliber gun was unfired and all six bullets were in the chamber.

With that Jack came out of his bedroom yawning and stretching. He looked at the sheriff suspiciously and reached for his gun. But the deputies were ready for trouble and covered Jack with rifles.

Willy mentioned that Jack had had a beef with the dead gunman. The sheriff looked at Jack who admitted he knew who the Kid was but had never actually met him. The sheriff approached Jack and slipped his gun from its holster. This gun had been fired and two empty .45 caliber cartridges were in the chamber. Jack glared at Willy who merely looked down at the floor.

When the sheriff found blood on Jack's boots he arrested Jack for murder and apologized to Willy.

f_t

A territorial judge presided at Jack's trial. But neither Broken Rock nor Santa Fe had a lawyer. Finn asked the banker, Derrick Collins, to represent Jack. Collins really hadn't liked Jack at all but a fee is a fee, he thought. He actually argued several points convincingly.

First, there was lack of motive. He told the jury that Jack had no argument with the Kid. In fact, he had never met him. Collins produced several witnesses who verified it. That didn't necessarily prove that Jack didn't know him but it seemed to cast some doubt.

Then he argued Jack's reputation with a gun. Why would he shoot someone in the back when he could face him down? And finally he argued that Jack wasn't stupid. Why would he walk in the dead man's blood? For a banker, he made a decent lawyer.

But the jury didn't care. Jack had bullied and stolen from many of them. They returned a guilty verdict in minutes and adjourned to the saloon for a drink to celebrate. Jack was sentenced to hang the next day.

ft

As Jack was led from the jail to the gallows, a man ran up to the sheriff and yelled at him to wait; there was a witness. Not hearing or caring, Jack made a desperate attempt to get away. He used his size to knock a deputy off of his feet.

Jack grabbed the key from the deputy's belt and undid the cuffs. He jumped on a passing horse, knocking the rider to the ground. As he fled out of town, the sheriff shot him twice, once in the right arm and once in the left leg.

The sheriff and a posse gave chase. They followed Jack to the foothills of the mountains.

Facing the posse were box canyons, steep hills and rugged terrain. They hadn't had time to provision for a long and difficult search. Far ahead they could see vultures circling overhead. They were sure their man was a goner and returned to Santa Fe.

Back in town, a witness to the shooting of the Santa Fe Kid had come forth. He had been too frightened to testify at the trial. But his conscience would not let an innocent man hang. He had been on the trail near the Kid's camp that night. He had heard two shots and hid behind a tree.

He had seen Willy ride off towards the Becker ranch. The territorial judge convened a hearing to consider this new evidence. And he took his time, wanting to do the right thing. The witness was positive he had seen Willy leaving the Santa Fe Kid's camp.

But there were questions on the judge's mind. What was this fellow doing out in the middle of the night? Did he have a beef with the Kid? How could he be so sure of an identification made in the dark of night? On the other hand, the evidence against Jack had been overwhelming even though that fellow Collins had raised valid questions.

In the end, the judge let Jack's conviction stand. Jack was dead. He had been a bad man but never a murderer until now. But the judge knew that bad behavior escalates and Jack could easily have had a motive. And would justice be served by hanging Willy? He certainly had a motive but the judge was certain that Willy would never kill again, even if he had committed murder that night.

So Willy was a free man as he rode along with Finn towards Broken Rock and home. They stopped to water their horses at the river. Finn was distracted; he hadn't said a word all the way home. Stepping off his horse, he motioned for Willy to do the same.

Father and son sat on two of the rugged stones. Finn looked at his son with a breaking heart. He knew what really happened that night. He had heard Willy in Jack's room. He had seen him saddle his horse and ride out. He followed Willy to the camp and had heard the shots. He had even seen the witness pass by.

Finn sat quietly for a few minutes but finally spoke to his son.

"When I saw you frame Jack I held my tongue. Jack deserved to be behind bars. He had hurt a lot of people in the area. He was arrogant and mean. He disrespected his mother, ignored me, and terrorized you, his own brother, for years. Jack evaded both the law and justice for a long time. But you, Willy, are a killer, a cold blooded killer."

Finn knew he had failed his son. But he also knew Willy did not have to turn to murder. Finn would have helped him stand up to the Kid; his ranch hands would have helped too. Instead Willy had taken the coward's approach and shot the man in the back.

Then Finn told Willy that it was time for him to leave the ranch and try to live with himself.

Willy was speechless. Stunned. His father had let Jack die so he could go free. But his father knew he had committed murder. He was petrified of leaving home. He did a good job on the ranch and earned what his father paid him. Where would he go? What would he do?

Finn sadly shook his head and remounted his horse. His rode alone towards home and Hanna.

A few months later the Becker's got word that Willy was dead. He had shot a man in the back over a woman. The dead man's brother called him out and shot him dead. Justice, many had said.

Finn stood by the rail of the corral with a cup of cold coffee in his hands. He was staring absently at the distant mountain peaks. Hanna walked from the house to her husband. Gently she took his hand and wept on his shoulder.

"We have lost everything," she whispered.

"But we still have each other," he responded.

The sadness in her eyes hurt to her very soul. The tears dried on her checks. She bowed her head, turned and slowly walked back towards the house. Finn tossed the dregs of his coffee onto the ground and followed his wife.

ft

Jack's remains were found days later. There was not enough left to bury. The buzzard sat on a nearby rock and watched as the posse rode off.

He had nothing to say.

–The End–

Randal Schmidt

Randal William Schmidt is a teacher, illustrator, and the author of *The Lands Beyond the Moon*, a fantasy novel. He is also the editor of a special classroom edition of *The Wonderful Wizard of Oz* by L. Frank Baum. He holds a Bachelor of Arts in English and History from Texas A&M University. He currently teaches Creative Writing and Literature at a Catholic college preparatory school in Texas. He and his wife, Brett, live near Dallas with their two children, James and Emilia. You can contact R.W. Schmidt by email: rwschmidtbooks@gmail.com

Comida

by Randal Schmidt

Leslie Parker woke to the cold steel of a gun barrel in his cheek. A voice like a pissed off rattlesnake spit in his ear.

"Levantarse."

A kick in the gut.

"Levantarse."

"Sí," he grunted back, "I'm getting up." The gun barrel pulled back from his face.

Les opened his eyes and wished he hadn't. He was a long way from Arizona.

The other man's face filled his vision. Lines like parched river beds cut across the pock marked skin. Black scruff with flecks of dried blood covered the jaw and the fat below the chin. His features were Spanish mixed with Yaqui Indian, a true Mexican of Sonora.

Yet, he was unlike any man that Les had ever encountered; there was wildness in his eyes that defied reason.

"Desayuno?" said Les, knowing it was futile. He'd get no breakfast. The dirt in his mouth was all he'd eaten in four days.

"Food? Comida?"

His captor didn't even bother to answer him. The bastard had had his breakfast before waking him.

Les pulled himself to his feet, feeling much older than his twenty-nine years. Four days of sleeping on Sonoran dirt made a man sore in every muscle.

The sun had newly risen, but the sky stayed gray and dead. Winter in northern Mexico. Les had almost frozen in his sleep. As the Mexican pulled himself up on his horse, Les stumbled towards his own.

He put his hand on the saddle and pressed his face into this beast. Its smell filled his nostrils and the warmth of it gave him a fleeting moment of comfort. Then, with effort, Les pulled back and swung himself into the saddle.

"Where we going?" His voice dripped with hatred. No answer. "A dónde vamos?"

The Mexican laughed—a guttural sound—and leveled the revolver at his chest. Intricate engravings twisted around the barrel, and the cylinder was likewise decorated. Somewhere beneath the filthy hand, the letters LP were etched into the walnut handle. The gun had been a gift from Ellie, Les's wife.

Late wife.

Yanking hard on his reins, the Mexican spun his horse away.

Les followed after him with no idea the direction or the destination. He'd have killed the Mexican in his sleep if he knew where they were or how to get back. But he had no desire to die slowly of starvation, lost in the desert.

He rode on, slouched in defeat. All he was leaving behind was a burned homestead back in the states.

His mind was emptied. He sensed motion and sound and smell, but they were as disconnected as his thoughts. Rise and fall in the saddle. Biege land. The revolver jingling on the Mexican's belt. A gritty wind on his face.

The horses plodded over the desert, snorting in the cold dawn. December of nineteen hundred and eleven. Not sure of the date.

The only food for miles was in a satchel slung over his captor's shoulder, some unidentifiable meat that the Mexican gnawed on as they rode. He would reach idly inside the leather and pull out a piece of it raw. Tearing at it like an animal, blood and spit running down his face.

Les was starving; hungry enough that even the satchel's contents were starting to seem appetizing. Maybe he'd be fed soon. If the Mexican was going through the trouble of hauling him along, he wouldn't just let Les die in the saddle. Would he?

When Les had first woken up, he'd thought the Mexican was a revolutionary, maybe one of Villa's boys. It was rare that they'd come across the border into Arizona, but not unheard of. The Parker homestead was close enough for such a raid.

But the two men had ridden for so long and seen no others—neither revolutionaries nor federales—that Les began to think the man might be something altogether different. Les had a reasonable grasp of Spanish, but no matter what language he asked in, he could get no answers from the man.

He had no choice but to follow him. Even if he somehow killed the Mexican and escaped, there were only miles of nothing as reward. Sonora was a big graveyard, and Les didn't want to pick out a plot just yet.

They rode for hours and hours without speaking. At all times, they were headed toward the mountains. With each hoof fall, the peaks grew larger on the horizon and the land became uneven. After a while, a jagged wall loomed in front of them. Where the snow clung to rock, they were white blades cutting into the sky. It was late in the day. The sky had grown a deeper gray and hinted of more snow in the night.

To Les, the mountains looked like pearly gates, and he was not eager to see them open. When his captor pulled up on the reins at the crest of a small rise, he motioned for Les to do the same.

The Mexican chewed on a piece of the stringy meat, drooling into his beard. When he smiled at Les, the broken teeth were stained red and yellow. He pointed up to a high ridge. Les followed his finger, but there was nothing to be seen there.

When he turned back, he looked at the revolver on the Mexican's belt and the bag of meat. Les was close enough that he could throw himself into the man, knock him from the saddle, wrest the gun from him and kill him.

The Mexican still had his eyes fixed where he'd pointed, but Les was putting his weight on his left stirrup to throw himself hard to the right. The Mexican spurred his horse on and out of reach.

The moment was lost.

The road led up and up, and Les's head throbbed with pain and delirium. He slipped into the steel grip of despair, and his mind beat against his skull.

Waking dreams flashed before him.

He saw blue eyes in a smoke-filled room. Lifeless and staring at the ceiling.

Ellie was as beautiful in death as in life, the only blemish a gash in her porcelain throat. Her shapely hand splayed on the floor. A diamond glistening in a gold band on her delicate finger.

After that, the Mexican's boot had stomped on Les's face. When he'd woken up, everything was gone. His house was burned, his own gun was facing him and he was being marched into the desert.

Why didn't the Mexican just leave him for dead, and take what loot there was?

Something didn't make sense, but Les's mind was in no shape to figure it out. He was back in the present now, and he slumped in his saddle as he followed the Mexican up the mountain road. The sound of hooves on rock and the squishing of the meat in the man's teeth mixed in the air.

Les leaned to his side, and his stomach heaved but without food, only bile came up.

How much farther could they go? The road became narrower, snaking back and forth, rising up to a hidden pass. At the top of the road, the pass was long and only wide enough for one horseman at a time. Les followed the Mexican. Halfway through was another cleft in the rock, and the Mexican turned off to the left into that other path.

Les thought he could see a pillar of smoke in front of him, but the pain in his head made all sight suspect, so he couldn't be sure. He turned away into the side path as well.

The Mexican said over his shoulder, "We go other way, other time, para comida."

Then, he laughed the same sick laugh as before, tore a piece of meat in his teeth and rode on. The path twisted back and after a while, the wall of rock on the left side fell away and revealed a sprawling vista. Les realized that he was looking out at the land they'd been riding over for days. They were high on the ridge that the Mexican had pointed out earlier.

The path ducked back under an outcrop of rock and finally into a cave. This, at last, was their destination.

The Mexican dismounted, pulled Les out of his saddle and dragged him into the cave. The sun had just set, but the cave provided shelter from the whipping mountain wind. The Mexican shoved him to the ground, went back out and reentered, holding a torch.

The light danced around the cave and revealed it to be larger than Les had expected. It had obviously been lived in for a long time and was furnished too, in the way an animal's den might be called furnished. The Mexican had a straw bed and a flat stone slab for a table, but little else.

The Mexican was pointing Les's revolver at him again.

"Go to sleep," he said, and Les, whether he wanted to or not, followed his order immediately. The hard day's ride and the continuing lack of food made him pass out almost as soon as he lay down.

When he woke, the torch had burned out but the sun's light reached into the cave. The Mexican was watching him, chewing on more of the meat and muttering something in incoherent Spanish or Yaqui.

Les pulled himself up to a sitting position and rubbed his bloodied face. He had dreamed of Ellie and heard his young wife's gentle laughter in his sleep, and when he awoke, the urge to take revenge upon the Mexican had been overwhelming. But with the gun still focused on him, revenge would have to wait.

"Can I have some food?" Les said, "Please, comida, dear Lord, comida."

The Mexican shook his head slowly, purposefully, and said, "No."

Les kicked at the dirt, but the Mexican sat motionless.

"What the hell do you want from me?"

"Comida," said the Mexican and broke into grunting laughter that rose in pitch until he sounded like a crazed coyote yipping in the cave. Les put his head down. The man was mocking him. But Les didn't give up right away. He wanted some answers.

"Who are you?" he said, "Why Arizona? Why'd you do it?"

In halting English, the Mexican said:

"I the Devil. I like to travel. I like variety. Variedad."

He smiled that hideous smile again, and Les wanted nothing more than to kick in what was left of those nasty teeth. He stopped asking questions, because anything the Mexican said only made Les want to kill him more.

The rest of that day passed without event, except that the Mexican got up and went out a few times, but never long enough for Les to do anything to help his situation.

Sundown found the two of them in the same position, Les sitting on the ground and the Mexican chewing and chewing at the meat, with the engraved revolver in his hand.

"Mañana," muttered the Mexican to himself, and Les did not like the sound of it, "Tomorrow."

Les was weak and drifted out of consciousness into a fitful sleep on the floor of the cave. During the night, he saw Ellie again, and his heartbreak was such that anything, even death, seemed a relief.

Just before dawn, still in the midst of dreams, Les rolled over on his side, and the uneven floor jabbed him in his cheek and woke him up. His right arm was extended, and he realized that he was clutching a loose rock, jagged all over and large enough that he could just get his hand around it.

The Mexican was still snoring. Les tightened his grip on the rock. He would not sit around and wait anymore. He would not take orders from the man who murdered his wife. He would have revenge, come what may.

In one motion, Les rolled and flung the rock as hard as he could at the Mexican. It struck the man in the throat and the revolver clattered to the ground. The Mexican awoke sputtering. By the time he realized what had happened, Les had rushed forward with what strength he had left. He grabbed the ornate gun.

The gun that Ellie had given him.

The gun that shook the cave when it fired.

The gun that killed the Mexican with one shot.

The dead man slid back into the straw bed. It had happened quickly. Now Les was alone in the cave, still hungry and still with no knowledge of where he was or who he had just killed.

The satchel of meat was on the floor. Les picked it up, left the dead man lying, went out and managed to pull himself onto a horse. He took the reins and followed the narrow path back to the mountain pass.

Les turned the other way to where he thought he'd seen smoke a day ago. He opened the satchel, but as hungry as he was, the smell from within was so pungent that he could not eat.

He was exhausted and unsteady in the saddle, but it didn't take him long to travel the length of the pass. At the other end, he saw what he'd hoped for.

Down below was the dusty outline of a Sonoran village.

The horse made the descent easily enough, but Les was so weak by then that at the outskirts of the village, he fell from his mount into the dirt, still clutching the Mexican's satchel.

An old man and his son came running out from a house and knelt beside him. The old man pulled Les to his feet and alternating between broken Spanish and broken English, the two men tried to converse.

"Please, señor, comida," begged Les, "Food, por favor." The old man sent his son running back into the house. More villagers were coming to see what the excitement was about.

When Les struggled to explain that he'd escaped from the mountains, the old man interrupted him and exclaimed:

"Diablo!"

He crossed himself and looked fearfully up at the pass. Les tried to speak, but the old man shook his head frantically, pointed back at the mountains and cried out:

"El caníbal! El caníbal!"

Les understood it all—the last week suddenly made sense—and he cried out to God as he dropped the satchel. When it hit the ground, the contents spilled out.

There in the Sonoran dirt was a diamond glistening in a gold band on her delicate finger.

–The End–

Steve Myers

Born in the hills of Pennsylvania and grew up in Ohio. Served in USAF in Southeast Asia during the Vietnam War and went to Kent State on the G.I. Bill. Published short stories, poetry, and novels, including the western *Along Showdown River*.

Captain Boylan's Raiders

by Steve Myers

We never knew where he came from and never found out his last name. I said, "What do they call you?"

And he said, "Jay."

I says, "Jay what?"

And him: "Just Jay."

Just Jay—I ask you, what kind of name is that?

Anyways, he just pops up out of the woods, out of nowhere, there the other side of the crick—him with that Henry rifle and on that big black horse, the horse still as a rock and its horse-skin, its hide, almost shinin' there in the light through the trees. Me and Vern was racin', our scrawny horses near dead, wheezin'—you know that harsh heavy wheezin'—and them damn bluebellies near on us, right on our ass as we turned off the road and rushed into that crick splashin' high sprays of water—it was then that we saw him on that big black with the rifle raised and we figured that sure as hell it was all over for us.

See, back then me and Vern rode with Captain Boylan from Clay County.

You know how it was with all that raidin' and burnin' and hoorahin' those damn Kansas Free-Soilers. Vern and me was second cousins—him near fifteen years older—and he got me in the troop oncet the real war started. Vern goes back to the Border Wars, you know. And he was in that big fight there at Wilson's Crick.

I didn't get into the fun until '62. I tell you, we was in some mean fights and we burned us many a cabin and shot hell out of many damn sympathizers and traitors, those we didn't hang. Then when the big war was over—at least when they said it was over—Captain says to us—there was maybe near fourteen to fifteen of us then—he says, "Robert E. Lee might surrender but I'll be damned to hell if I will."

Well, then we went on a couple small raids—a warehouse, a cross-roads horse station, nothin' much—and only that big one at Graeter's Station where the Federals were waitin' and we lost two and the Captain's brother Robert takes the Kennedy boys and lights out to pull a raid up to Kay-ro. So there's just eight of us by then—and we stopped to rest at old Pop Farrell's place and he gave us a good feed and put us up and the next day when everybody got up to go Vern said us two would stay over if the Captain didn't mind and meet up later at Bracken's sister's place. Captain winked at us and set off and the rest followed him along the trail to the road. You see, Old Pop had two sweet things stayin' there with him and his old woman to help with chores and Vern and me figured we'd try them out. Vern says to me, "Nothin' like them young ones when they's fresh and juicy." And Pop didn't seem to mind as long as that store whiskey we stole held out.

So the next mornin' at dawn, the light pale through the chinks in the barn, and the two of us tangled there with a beauty a piece and layin' there in the soft and sweet smell of the hay when I heard their horses and I looked out a hole there in the boards and saw them comin' into the yard—maybe six of them—and I kicked Vern and we hardly had time to git on our trousers and boots and drop down from the loft to our horses. We just had time to bridle them and the hell with the saddle and we bust out the back at full tilt, hell bent—and we even left our pistols and the carbine Vern took from that bluebelly we bushwhacked outside Sedalia.

They heard us of course and they was hot after us and zingin' bullets over our heads. They chased us cross the field and jumped the rail fence and was gainin' until we hit that road and our Missouri ponies left them way behind. We was feelin' good and laughin' about it when there at the fork—the one just this side of Red Horse crossing—there was six more bluebellies and they started for us with fresh horses.

And, like I said, they was hard on our ass when we splashed through that crick and the kid showed up—popped up like the devil or an Injun or a ghost. He raises that rifle and he fires right past my head. I mean, I heard that bullet zing by—hell, I felt it clip some hair. So we stopped—the both of us—and raised our hands because we knew it was over and maybe—since they was regulars—they wouldn't hang our sorry asses.

But then there's that flash and loud crack near in our faces—and the shot went past again. And then I understood and just glanced back to see two federal horses down on the ground and riders tumblin' and the others hightailin' it back to the road.

So me and Vern kicked our ponies in the ribs and rode by the kid—him pale-faced and cold lookin' like a slab of cut stone and blue eyes cold as river ice and coal black hair chopped below the ears like it been cut with a knife or dull shears. And him not even old enough to have a beard—just peach fuzz, if that—sittin' there on that big black, a glove on his left hand under the barrel, shootin' at those bluebellies as they took off like scalded dogs.

Vern and me waited there at the edge of the woods and he come up to us and Vern says, "Kid, we sure do appreciate your help."

But he didn't say a thing.

I says, "It was smart, shootin' the horses."

He gave me that stone look was all. Tight lipped, the kid was—I mean, the most he ever said at one time was there at the end when he rode off.

And then I asked him his name and all we got was "Jay."

f$_t$

So we took him on—or, if the truth be told, he took us on, since he had corn cakes there in that sack on his saddle and a canteen full of fresh water and that Henry rifle. We rode down along the green river—I think they calls it the James—and then we cut west and toward sundown we come out of the woods to Bracken's sister's place. She was a widow with one youngster—a towhead boy about five—and I thought she had a nice face and pretty in her way even if she were a might stringy. There was a cabin built of rough board and a chicken coop in the back and a ramshackle building that was supposed to be a stable or a barn. No doubt her old man—now dead from some fever for three years—wasn't any kind of carpenter.

Well, the Captain was there and Bracken and Sid Reynolds. I told how the kid had saved our skins and all and Captain looked him over and then asked, "You want to join us in our fight against tyranny?"

The kid just looked back at the Captain with those cold eyes and nothin' showin' on his face.

"Well," Captain says, "you joinin' us in the fight?"

"I already have," the kid says.

"Good," Captain says, "now let's us get some supper."

That night the Captain and Bracken and Reynolds slept in the cabin. Knowin' Reynolds, I figure he comforted the widow in the night. Vern and me slept on a pile of hay in that barn while the kid lay on the ground near his horse, his rifle beside him.

I want to tell you somethin' about that kid and horses. You wouldn't've thought it—him shootin' those Federals' horses—but him and horses had somethin' special. Of course, before he did anythin' else he took care of that black—watered it, fed it, wiped it down, checked its hoofs, and talked to it soft and easy like in no language I ever heard—if it was a language at all, except horse talk. Then he did that with all the horses. He'd stroke the face, drawin' a line down the front to the nostrils, and pet it and sort of hum into its ear and in no time that horse would follow him around like a puppy.

Even the Captain said the kid had a gift from Nature herself or the Lord.

Anyways, the next mornin' the rest showed: Bud Whittaker, Big Bill Burns, and Rhodes. They said the Moyer twins lit out for Texas and maybe meet up with Price in Mexico. Vern told them about the kid and how he saved us and they was impressed—except for Rhodes. You see, Rhodes was just naturally ornery and he had a real nasty mean streak.

Some said he got it from his old man but I knew his mam and I say he come by it from both the acorn and the oak. I mean, we all did some things we never would tell our mothers—things like takin' scalps and hangin' them on the bridle—Bloody Bill Anderson was big for that—and knots in a cord for each one we kilt—but I quit that right quick because there was things not to remember.

But Rhodes enjoyed it all—too much. The killin', the burnin', the hangin', and all pleasured him so much he couldn't get enough. He loved to set things afire—cabins, fields, people. He'd torch a cabin and watch it burn while the folks ran and he'd cackle like a crazy rooster. Oncet I saw him run down a boy no more than seven or eight, run the boy over with his horse.

Well, Rhodes said that killin' horses was nothin' much and it didn't prove the kid could shoot. So he got on the kid and called him Dead-eye and Fuzz Face and such. So the third day we was there, the kid takes up his rifle and shoots an apple off a tree there at the edge of the woods.

Rhodes says, "How we know he meant to hit that? Could be Fuzz Face was aimin' at the tree or the whole damn woods."

The kid gives Rhodes that stone look—like the next one would be in Rhodes—and then suddenly ups his rifle and fires and knocks an apple loose and before it hits the ground he works the lever and shoots again and blasts that apple to pieces.

Vern says, "Hey, Zeb, what's the kid got agin apples?"

"Them's sour and gnarly," I says, "like some people—and good for nothin'."

Rhodes says, "And where the hell he get that rifle? Had to stolen it—a rifle like that. See how it goes 'gainst a real rifle in a real fight, not agin apples. Henry's no damn good outen hundred yards or so."

Vern says, "Sour apples and sour grapes, as the fella says."

And from the cabin doorway the Captain says, "Well, now we know who covers the retreat."

Because, you see, the Captain had a plan. After that little affair in Liberty back in February, the Captain figured robbin' Federal banks was the way to go. He said, "That money is rightfully ours even if it is greenbacks." So the idea was to pick a fat bank somewheres and then hit a warehouse or such for supplies and then hole up for the winter down there towards the Ozarks where there was a good place and his brother Robert could join us there.

First off, we had to pick us a bank. The Captain says we'd scout it out like a raid. So he tells Reynolds to take a wagon and the widow and the boy and pretend like they was a family lookin' for somewheres to settle down. He gave him most all the money we had.

Rhodes says, "How you know he'll come back? What if he just takes off with the bitch and her pup and the cash?"

"All right," the Captain says, "we'll keep the boy here."

So they left and we waited. We found things to do—patch up clothes, clean our revolvers, stuff like that—I found me an old saddle in the barn and worked on that—but Rhodes gets antsy. He starts on the kid—pickin' on him, pokin' him in the back with a stick and then lookin' away—that kind of thing—and he says to the kid, "You keep your hands off my horse."

Because by now all the horses was the kid's pets. He didn't care much for people's company but he sure got along with horses. And there was one other thing: sometimes you'd catch him reading. He had some papers—looked like pages from a book—there was maybe ten of 'em and they was scorched, burnt at the edges. But if he saw you watchin' he'd put those papers back in his shirt pocket.

Rhodes said he was goin' to git those papers and see what they was all about. Vern says, "What good is that to you? You can't read a lick."

And then the Captain says, "You all leave that boy alone. Those pages he's studyin' are from the Good Book. I tell you to leave him alone."

We did—but mostly because the kid stayed by hisself. That lasted a week at most before Rhodes come up with his crazy idea. See, there was a crick runnin' back of the place and there was a spot where it widened into a pool. That was where the kid would wash. I mean that kid was just about the cleanest person I ever saw. He washed everyday—with soap—and two or three times a week he'd strip down naked and wash his whole body. Anyways, it was a bright warm day near the end of September and the kid out to the crick to wash. Rhodes says, "Boys, come watch some fun—I'm goin' to fix that Fuzz Face."

So we followed him, stayin' back some yards, and he went to the crick where it was set off behind some bushes and a tree and he took off his boots and all his clothes so he was naked. That was one ugly sight, I tell you. Rhodes was all hair from his straggle beard and down his chest and back—like a bear almost. Then he pushed through the bushes and we come up to see.

The kid was stark naked there in the pool, the water just over his knees, and he'd just dunked his head 'cause his hair was all wet and he was shakin' it like a dog does to throw off the water. Just then Rhodes jumps in behind the kid and grabs the kid from behind and bends the kid over, pushin' his head down, forcing the kid down so his face is in the water. And then Rhodes begun to mount the kid, usin' him like you would some woman—but from the back end. At first we laughed because we thought it was a joke, you know. But Rhodes kept at it—squeezin' the kid's neck and pushin' him into the water with one hand and trying to force himself on the kid with the other.

And then the kid retched down into that crick and come up with a rock and spun round and hit Rhodes upside the head. Rhodes staggered back and the kid stepped into him and swung and hit him again so hard blood come gushin' out of Rhodes's nose and out his ear. He fell back onto the bank with his feet still in the water.

The kid scrambled to his gear in a pile on the bank and he pulled out a knife, a big thick long one—like a Bowie knife. He come over to Rhodes layin' there moanin' and the blood still pourin' out and the kid with that stone look as he bent down and we figured he was goin' to slit Rhodes's throat or even gut him.

And then we heard the Captain say, "That's enough."

He come through us and went to Rhodes and the kid and he brought up his revolver and cocked it and he said again—this time straight to the kid—"That's enough, son, stand back."

The kid rose up and stepped back a little. He didn't drop the knife and he didn't look scared—he didn't look anythin'—he just stood there with water dripping from his hair.

The Captain looked down at Rhodes and says, "One thing to do such to a pig but to the boy—that's the sin of Sodom." And then he pulls the trigger and puts a forty-four slug into Rhodes's chest. Rhodes coughs maybe twice before he dies.

The Captain says to the rest of us—but not to the kid—he says, "Go git a shovel and put him in a hole. Not near the buildings or the water—out there in the woods."

When the Captain leaves Vern says, "Well, I guess the kid gets Rhodes's horse."

"He don't want it," I says.

So Vern says, "I guess it's mine then."

ft

While we waited for Reynolds and the widow to come back the little towhead took up with the kid. In no time the kid had the boy up on that big black gelding, the boy hangin' on to the kid around the waist as they rushed across the field and through the deep grass and it was bareback too. It was somethin' to see—that boy's hair streamin' behind him and his face just shinin'.

It was nigh on three weeks at least before Reynolds and the widow come back. I was sure glad because Vern did the cookin' and he was good at a lot of things that required ridin' or shootin' but a pistol nor saddle can't make a meal. Hell, even his coffee ruint your guts.

Now the kid and the little boy did all right on fish from the crick and rabbits they snared and sometimes they'd share with us—and the kid even made flapjacks—don't ask me how he knew but they was damn good compared to Vern's. I mean Vern even burnt flapjacks or he used too much water and made a soggy mess. But most of the time we had dried soup beans—what there was and there wasn't much—and chunks of old dried hog meat—that what was left from the year before—and fried corn meal that was burnt. Some of us thought about butcherin' a horse— but no one was hungry enough or dumb enough to face that Henry rifle. So the first thing I thought of when I seen that wagon and that widow and the flour barrel and sugar sack and that slab of bacon in the wagon— the first thing I thought of was my belly.

Anyways, Reynolds gives his report and the short of it was there was no banks worth botherin' about nowheres close. But there was a regular Federal supply wagon that carried a payroll sack oncet a month to the troop holed in at Sullivan's Station. The escort was only four bluebellies and a driver and a guard in the wagon.

"When's the next trip?" the Captain says.

"Friday after next," Reynolds says.

f_t

So on that Friday mornin' we was ready at dawn—sittin' there on our horses in the cool mornin', the horses snortin', horse breath and man breath hangin' in the air. The Captain comes out in his officer's coat with the three copper bars on the collar and his hat with the gold and black cord and his revolver in the holster on his left side and his boots glistenin' in that early light. He mounted his horse and waved to the widow and her boy in the doorway with the yellow light from the table lamp behind them.

The Captain says, "All right, boys, let us do our duty like men and as God intended and show no mercy."

We followed along the trail until we come on a twisty wagon road of deep ruts and high grass and then we hit the good road between Palmyra and Sullivan's Station. To tell the truth, we all had been on many a raid and nobody was scared and we was lookin' for a fight of some kind 'cause our blood was up, you know, needin' the action. And the ride was a pretty one with the sun comin' up through the trees now full of color—red and yellow and the sumac bright as fire—and the air sweet smellin' from the dew and the high white grass at the side of the road.

About noon we got to a spot where there was a sharp curve you couldn't see around and there was thick woods on either side. So Vern and Bracken takes their axes and fells a tree across the road. Then we all get into the woods, split half and half 'cept for the kid. The Captain sent him up the road a ways with his rifle. He tells the kid, "You don't shoot less it goes bad. If so, I count on you to save us."

The kid nodded and then went up there and hid his horse in the woods and got settled in some bushes.

The Captain says to me, "No need for him to stain his soul with killin' unless he has to."

Maybe an hour, maybe less, we hear the horses and the creak of the wagon. There was two bluebellies joggin' up front and then the supply wagon with a arched canvas top with a driver in a blue blouse and no hat and workin' his mouth like he had a chaw and the guard asleep beside him and then ten yards or so behind the wagon come two troopers runnin' their mouths about somethin'.

So they go past and start around the bend and suddenly one of the front troopers shouts, "Hold on! Hold! Damn tree in the way."

Just then me and Vern and Bracken charge out from the woods firin' our pistols at the two in the rear. Before they git a chancet to turn 'round they's dead, shot off their horses. The two in front hear the shots and come hellin' with pistols drawn, rushin' at us.

It's then Reynolds, Bud, and Big Bill charge out behind them with revolvers blazin' and those two are shot off their horses and the horses keep on runnin', followin' the other two down the road.

The Captain comes out of the trees and shoots the guard twicet before he even wakes up and he tumbles out onto the ground. The driver stands up and raises his hands like he was surrenderin'. Reynolds turns his horse 'round and comes up to the wagon and the Captain nods and Reynolds raises his revolver and shoots the driver in the back of his head and he falls forward with that plug of tobacco shootin' straight out of his mouth. Then the Captain whistles and waves to the kid and in no time he's on the black and comin' toward us.

We strip the bluebellies of boots and trousers and revolvers—they had those '58 Remingtons—before we drug them into the woods—but we didn't scalp 'em, although Big Bill thought we should. The Captain checks the wagon and says there's supplies aplenty and cartridges and caps and barrels of salt pork and flour and corn meal and slabs of bacon and blankets and rope and a crate of Spencer carbines and even a copper-lined keg of coal oil. But no payroll.

The Captain says, "Men, the Lord provides. We have enough now to last the winter and rest up while I plan the spring campaign."

Reynolds wanted to know if we was goin' to stop by and pick up the widow and her boy.

The Captain shakes his head and says, "We can't go back there now. The Federals will scour the earth for us, and best if we keep away from there."

"But," Reynolds says, "what will she do?"

The Captain says, "Same as she did before us."

"But—" Reynolds starts.

And the Captain says, "Now you git in that wagon and turn it around—unless you desire that woman's flesh so much you would turn cowardly deserter."

Reynolds was stupid but he knew what that meant.

Well, we travel all day and set up camp way off the road, pullin' the wagon behind the trees and the Captain says no fires. Then we was up before dawn and another day on the road, drinkin' canteen water to wet the corn cakes. But not the kid—he'd cut off the road and dive into the woods and come back eatin' berries or nuts or ramps.

Vern says, "He got to be Injun. Who else knows all that and moves like that—huh?"

I says, "How many Injuns you see with face that pale and eyes that blue?"

The Captain was just ahead of us and he slows down until we're beside him and he says, "It is a true mystery the way that boy appeared. It was a sign. I wonder if he's an angel sent to help us on our way." After three days we come upon the first slopes and we mostly drug and pushed that wagon along the trail, over the rocks and ruts that was only a bobcat's idea of a trail. But finally we come on a pass that was more like a sideways slice into a hill and we passed through and there it was down below—a farm with a log cabin with a shake roof and a split-board barn big enough for both horses and cows and a fallin' down outbuildin' like for pigs and a crick runnin' the far side and the whole thing like a bowl set in the hills and the high hills beyond going up like steps to the mountains shinin' blue in the distance. And all of it set there in a blaze of red and yellow leaves.

The Captain says, "There it is—Cousin Roy's."

Cousin Roy was near fifty and scrawny, sickly scrawny, not work-hard scrawny if you know what I mean. He was glad to see us and the supplies. He was alone there 'cause the brain fever taken his wife and both daughters and he'd had a touch of it hisself and so was deaf in his right ear. And before that his sons Morgan and Earmon had gone off to the war and had never come back yet. And somethin' got to his chickens and a bear kilt his cow—ripped out her insides—and his pigs went wild there in the woods and he wasn't able to round 'em up.

Maybe most of that was true—I don't know. The Captain did say it sounded like the torments of Job.

Well, we settled in. Me and Vern in the loft in the barn, the kid with the horses, and the rest in that big cabin. We parked the wagon and carried the food inside but left the cartridges and the carbines and the coal oil because the air wouldn't hurt them none.

And the next day the kid was up at daybreak and out in them woods and trampin' the hills and he comes back with nuts and roots and such and brews himself a tea that was better than anything I drunk before. And he never et with us—he kept to himself and his horses—his, because there was no doubt nobody could handle them the way he could and Vern said that if the kid didn't give the nod nobody could even mount his own animal. The kid would cook his fish or rabbit or possum over his own fire and drink his tea and study those burnt pages of his.

Then one time he takes an old rusty scythe from the barn and rubs the blade over with some red-lookin' clay and a stone and then he gets a whetstone from his sack and sharpens that blade and then goes out into the field where there was that high white grass even in November and he cuts it all—the whole damn field—and brings it into the barn.

Cousin Roy shook his head at that. I mean, the rest of us just lazed around—but not the kid. Hell, he even took a loop of rope from horse to horse and—him on the black—led them all in a parade out of the barn and all around the place—the horses gentle and quiet and showin' off almost.

And next he gets an ax and a bar and he tears down that ramshackle outbuilding. Vern and me helped with that just to do somethin'. We split the sides and roof slabs and drove them into the ground to make a kind of fence or low stockade around the back of the cabin and the barn to keep out bears and such.

Then the air changed all of a sudden. The wind brought a hard rain and the leaves flew in bunches from the trees and at night there come a hard frost and in the mornin' the short grass was frozen and a thin top of ice lay in the water bucket. It was cold and the air was sharp like that for near a week and then all of a sudden we got bright sunshine and you'd think it was summer again. Everythin' dried out and we went on a hog hunt in the woods to get us a pig to roast and we got nothin' because they was too smart for us and took off before we could get a clear shot—except the one that run up behind Big Bill and knocked him flat on his ass. Of course, the next day a gutted hog was hanging upside down from the tree off to the side of the cabin and we all knew who had shot it and bled it and left it there for us.

And Vern says, "If he ain't no Injun, he should be."

And it was mid-day that we seen them comin' through the cut. There was young Robert Boylan and then the two Kennedys—you never seen a meaner pair, I tell you—and trailin' behind was a woman wearin' a slouch hat like she was a raider and her hair all straggly hangin' down.

The Captain was near to dancin' seein' his brother. They grabbed one another and talked at the same time and finally Cousin Roy says, "Let's celebrate. We got us a pig to roast and I got a fire inside."

And Robert says, "We confiscated twelve bottles of store whiskey from a store in Belleville that would go with that pig."

So we all went inside the cabin except for the kid who taken the horses and, when Robert asked about the kid, the Captain said the kid knew horses better'n anyone he ever seen. And—inside—Robert asks again about the kid and who he was and all and then Reynolds points to his head and Cousin Roy says, "He's tetched. Works hard as hell and makes a horse say its prayers but he's tetched."

So we set up a spit from an iron rod out of the wagon and the stands for the kettle and we set about roasting that pig and Robert opened three bottles of that store whiskey and Cousin Roy brought out one of the jugs of corn he was hidin' in the root cellar under the cabin and we had us a time.

Robert told about raidin' into Illinois and bustin' two banks and then on the way here they'd stopped off at a place outside St. Louis and "acquired the lovely lady you see there enjoyin' the whiskey."

The truth was she wasn't lovely. She had a kind of pug face and straggly brown hair with nary a curl but she was plump and friendly and when she laughed she showed all her teeth and none was rotten.

Well, after a while the kid comes in and sits quiet there against the wall by the door, legs crossed like an Injun. I wondered then about him—I mean, he never come inside. Maybe it was because of the woman—you never can tell about people when it comes to women. I mean, even myself, I get funny around one and look at her and think maybe she'd like a touch, you know.

Anyways, the kid was havin' none of the whiskey and Reynolds and Big Bill and the Kennedys took it wrong. But the Captain steps in and says, "The boy knows better than to succumb to temptation."

And then we told about the kid's shootin' and Robert says, "Well, I'm too drunk now but tomorra we'll have us a contest and do some real shootin'."

And the kid almost smiles—I mean, it was the first time I seen him show anythin' at all—except with the towhead, but that didn't count.

Then he says the most I'd heard from him in a long time—he says, "I will sure look forward to it, sir."

Then the Captain says, "Except for the Moyers and that Sodomite Rhodes, we are together again. Come spring we will bring God's wrath and hell's fury down on that spawn of Satan in the north."

We drank to that and the kid slipped out the door.

ℱ

Well, you can guess how the afternoon and the evenin' went. I don't recall how much of that pig was et but I do remember all the whoopin' and hollerin' and Cousin Roy got out his fiddle—which he couldn't play worth a dog—but nobody cared—and the fancy lady was up and dancin' and taken off her clothes piece by piece and we was cheerin' her on and Bud and Bracken takes her into the bedroom in the back—that cabin had four rooms and a loft—and by then my head was dull–like and my mouth was sour and my tongue was thick so I got up and headed for the barn.

Out in the night—how did it git dark so fast?—I staggered to the barn and I sees the kid standin' there lookin' up at the sky. I says, "Jay, what's you doin'?"

And he says, "Countin' the stars."

I looked up but got so dizzy I near fell flat. I heard the shouts and the fiddle from the cabin and smelled the burnin' pig in the smoke out the chimbley. Then in the light from the cabin window I saw a kind of frost floatin' in the air, shimmerin' and turnin' like in a wind as weak as your breath, and it settled on the kid's hair.

I went into the barn full of horses—the air thick with horse warmth and smell—and I climbed the ladder into the loft and flopped down on the hay. Sometime in the night I heard Vern come strugglin' and cursin' as he climbed the ladder.

And he says, "Why, even the Captain had some of that fancy woman."

And then he starts to snort and snore and I kicked him but it did no good. Sometimes you could stick straw in his mouth and he'll come awake coughin' and spittin' but that won't work when he's drunk—he'd just choke.

44

Later I woke and thought I heard the kid with the horses, movin' about down below, but I fell back asleep. The smell was what got me up—a thick chokin' smell like lamp oil burnin' and then I heard the cracklin' and a sound like a strong wind blowin'—but a wild wind—a kind of roar—and then I seen the flames runnin' up the back wall. I poked Vern and shook him full awake and yelled "Fire" into his ear and drug and pushed him to the ladder and he slid down to a clump on the floor. I jumped down and grabbed him and pulled him out into the yard and away from the barn.

It was dawn—the sun still below those hills to the east but the gray light was showin' through the trees and there was a cover of frost on the ground.

"Damn!" Vern says and we both turned to see the cabin roof all afire.

And there was flames a man high in a ring around the cabin where stacks of dry grass and hay burned. And flames snaked along the walls— the fire roarin' and stinkin' of coal oil. Thick logs is slow to burn even soaked with oil—they just smolder and smoke—but that roof was shake and there was straw to keep in the heat in winter. And there was that ring of flames everywhere 'cept at the door. Then we seen that the fence was burnin' and makin' a wall of fire all across the back and no way could you run through there. Even the outhouse was near gone—just a dark shape in the yellow flames.

The first one out of the cabin was the Captain in his winter under- wear and bootless and coughin' and shakin' his head. Behind him come the lady with a blanket around her down to her naked legs. Then Robert, stark naked but wearin' boots, rushes out and knocks the lady flat down to the ground. Then I seen the flash across that open clear field the kid had mowed and I heard the crack just as the Captain grabbed his chest, opened his mouth like to shout an order, and fell face-forward to the ground. And right smack after that the second shot got Robert square in the forehead and he dropped like a pole-axed pig.

I looked across that field and saw the kid there at the edge of the woods, the woods a stagger of bare trees. Him on that black horse—that horse as still as a statue—and all the other horses in a string there—the lead one tied to a tree—and their breaths and the smoke from the rifle like a mist around them.

There was yellin' and screams that cut through my head comin' from the cabin and two more come out in underwear—Bracken and Reynolds—and the kid comes forward out of the gun smoke and gets them one shot on top of the other. Then the Kennedys in boots and trousers and revolvers in their hands—and one runs left and the other right—but that didn't help them 'cause the kid moves closer and nails one in the head and the other in the back and he fell and kicked and started to crawl and the kid put one in the side of his head and then they both lay there with their revolvers on the frost-crust.

The lady was on her hands and knees and shreikin' like a scalded cat and I begun to shake and liked to run but Vern grabs my arm and says, "No use. Just stand here and wait—he'll get 'round to us."

Then the cabin roof fell in and the screams stopped and no more come out. The cabin was all fire now with flames shootin' out between the logs and somethin' exploded and there was loud pops and the smell of burnin' flesh in the smoke. The lady was shiverin' and cryin' softly to herself and around her was six bodies layin' there not movin'—except for Reynolds, who twitched and lay on his side, holdin' in his guts. And Big Bill, Bud, and Cousin Roy were burnt up. So there was just fire and smoke behind us and the open field and the kid and his rifle in front.

Now he was on his horse and comin' toward us, the gun smoke driftin' behind him, his rifle across and restin' on the saddle, and his right hand still on it, still on the trigger. He come slow and steady—straight at us. He come too slow for me and I was about to run again—but there was nowhere to go.

That black stopped close enough I could feel his breath and see his eyes as hard as the kid's but black—hard not blue. The kid looks down at us for a second and then rides over to Reynolds moanin' there and he points that rifle right at Reynolds' head and fires and that black never moved, didn't flinch.

Then the kid rides up to us and he says, "Don't bury them."

Vern says, "We can't do that. That ain't Christian. Them wild hogs would come and et 'em."

The kid thinks about that for a spell and then he says, "Will you take care of her—the woman?"

Vern says, "We sure will."

46

The kid says, "I mean the right way. She's no dog to kick or beat."

"We'll do right by her," Vern says, "and treat her like a lady."

"Blankets and biscuits and dried rabbit is in the wagon," the kid says.

Then he starts to turn his horse and I says, "Jay?"

He looks back at me and says, "My pap called me that and so did my sis but my mam called me Jeremiah." Then he rides across the field— quicker now—and goes by the horses tied to the tree and then up the hill to the cut and was gone.

"Well," Vern says, "the sun's comin' up and we got a big enough fire to keep us warm until the frost is burnt off. And we got us a string of horses and a wagon and food and a crate of carbines and even a woman. We'll bury those ain't burnt and head out."

"Where to?" I asks.

Vern says, "Well, we can't stay here—this place is cursed."

I looked around at the fires and the bodies and I nodded.

Vern says, "It come over me that we should start west in the spring but in the meantime I thought you might care to comfort a young widow these comin' long winter nights and seein' I already have me a woman . . ."

"I like the sound of that," I says.

"So," Vern says, "that's where we're headed."

"And him," I says, "the kid—where you think he's headed?"

Vern laughs and as we walk over to the woman he says, "Him? Well, I suppose he's off to kill some more of our kind since he ain't all together sure which ones it was that done it—whatever it was. Yep, he's out to kill more of our kind—and he's sure as hell good at it."

"But," I says, "he didn't kill us."

And Vern: "You cain't never tell about people. Everybody's got a soft spot somewheres."

–The End–

Stuart Suffel

Stuart Suffel's body of "work" includes stories published by *Jurassic London, Evil Girlfriend Media, Enchanted Conversation: A Fairy Tale Magazine,* and *Aurora Wolf* among others. He exists in Ireland, lives in the Twilight Zone, and will work for Chocolate Sambuca ice cream.

Dealing From the Bottom

by Stuart Suffel

The swirl of dry dust which funneled up from the ground caused Jarak's colt to snort in distaste. Jarak patted its neck, partly to calm the animal, partly to calm himself.

"Easy Jade," he whispered to the nervous horse. The colt gave a soft neigh. He patted it again. He could not blame the colt. There was a taste to the dust. A taste of death and decay. The Deadlands outside Bolton favored neither man nor beast. It treated all with the same contempt.

He pulled his neckerchief up over his mouth, raised a hand to shade away the brightness and peered across the wide expanse. Nothing yet. He lifted the Henry out of its scabbard and gave it a quick inspection for any mud. There was none. Or if there had been, it had frazzled up in the heat on the way over from the river bed. He was tempted to open it up, check it all again. But that was foolishness. Nervousness, if he was honest. The rifle was as clean as it could be.

He looked again out to the wide open plain. Whatever died out here would eventually dissolve in the heat of the sun, or be picked clean by buzzards. The Deadlands might be an uncaring killer, but it cleaned up after itself. He only hoped it didn't take his prey.

He slid the repeater back into its holder. Six of them. One handgun between them, if old man Rudy was to be believed. Knife carriers the rest. Scum. Low-life, raping scum.

Old man Rudy. Skin as leathery as a lizard's and eyes to match, one of them blue and swollen, like a blue-bottle fly trapped in a hardboiled egg. Ancient, decrepit and half blind, he practically lived on the porch outside Lucy's Bordello. But he identified each one of them—right down to their boots. And for that Jarak was grateful.

For sure Sheriff Olsen took down all the details in his book. Their names, how they looked, how they dressed, how they rode. The old man was thorough. Jarak watched the sheriff write it all down, every word. And that's where it stayed. In the book.

He'd most likely hang for this. If they caught him, and they most likely would. Not too many half breeds in this part of the county. They'd hang him, but they'd beat him bad first. Indians don't kill white men. No matter what.

The horse neighed loudly. He realized he was holding the reins with a clenched fist. He quickly released his grip. Jade was all he owned in the world. That and the Henry. One earned, the other stolen. He'd never be allowed back to work with the smith. Not now. Not after stealing his rifle. Hanson was a fair enough man, once you worked hard and didn't answer back. But that was all over. A 'wild un' Jarak was now. 'Nothin' worse than an Injun turned' the white folks often said.

They were wrong. There was. Someone who was bought and sold like cattle. Less than a slave. A thing. To be used and abused as men chose. She did not choose. She did not choose then men who called at her room. No.

He did not pretend to know what love was. He had never known a woman's touch, felt a woman's breath upon his neck. But he knew kindness, and she was the only one who had ever looked at him with any. And he knew wrong. Yes. He knew that. And justice.

A pistol was useless against a rifle. A rifle he used every time the smithy let him, which was often enough to make shooting dead six desert-weary riders an easy task. It wasn't fair. There was no honor in it. But then, they didn't deserve any.

A form shimmered in the distance. A ball of black with a trail of smoky dust around it. He stared at the approaching shape—a mile at most away. It was them.

Would she know? Would someone tell her? They'd have to. The whole damned town would know. The whole damned county.

He clipped the colt over into the shadows of a nearby half-roofed stall. The afternoon sun still had some bite to it and so the horse neighed its thanks. He dismounted, threw the reins over a post and lifted the repeater out of its scabbard again. He felt its weight. It was already loaded. He ran his hand along the base of the barrel. It felt cool against his now-slightly-wet palm.

Mister Landon, the smithy, loved the Henry and Jarak understood why. It was beautiful. Elegant. And it did what was asked of it. Without question. Just as Jarak had these many years. With his free hand, he took the ragged cushion from under his saddle and set it down on a wooden post that ran along the roofed corral. He rested the Henry on the cushion and carefully jutted his shoulder against the butt to judge the height and the hold. It was perfect. He wiped his palm dry. Another five minutes at most.

Six men. Barrett, a red-haired drunk and the leader of the gang. Roberson, a known Army deserter and wife beater. Gerard, a thief, a liar and a slanderous cur, and his brother Jake, the same. The other two were hangers-on, Brant and Bakerfield, both convicted horse thieves. Always together, like the pack of dogs they were. Low-lifes all of them. But not as low as the girl they violated—not as far as Sheriff Olsen was concerned.

The black cloud drew closer. They were riding hard. Big poker game tonight, twenty tables. If they didn't arrive back in Bolton by sunset, they'd get no seat. Jarak smiled to himself. It was that piece of information, supplied by old man Rudy, that had sealed their fate. He carefully balanced the rifle on the cushion and walked over to his horse. He loosened the canteen from its satchel and took a long swig.

"Man should never leave his piece unattended," a voice said.

Jarak swung around, eyes wide with shock. But then he quickly relaxed. "What you doing here Rudy?" he asked. "I don't need no help."

The old man who had given him so much information gave a toothless grin back. The musket he held was an old one. Be lucky if it could reach ten paces. Jarak nodded to the musket with a smirk. "You'll be lucky to hit your own foot with that."

The old man grinned wider. "Ain't aiming for my feet young 'un." He lifted the rifle level to Jarak's stomach and fired. Jarak's middle exploded into a red mess. He hit the ground. The pain sent a wave of shock through his body, but not as much as the shock he felt in his mind. He sat and stared at the old man, his look a desperate question.

"Them six is customers, Injun. Good customers. Good 'nuff for Lucy to pay me a month's drinking money. Sheriff too."

Jarak drew in a breath, but it was his last. He slumped to the ground. Dead.

f_t

Some minutes later six horsemen pulled up to a half-roofed stall to see a face they knew.

"Hey, Rudy, what brings you out here?" the red-haired one asked the old man.

Rudy smiled. "Afternoon Barrett. A wild one," he said, pointing to a nearby young colt. "Escaped early this morning. Lucy asked me to tame it."

Barrett looked at the horse, then at the old man. The colt was saddled. The old man wasn't making sense. But then he never did. It was none of his business either way.

"Sure Rudy. You wanna ride back to Bolton with us?"

Rudy shook his head. "You boys ride on. Ye don't wanna be late. Tables are all set up. I've to do a bit of tiding up here first."

It was then Barrett noticed the spade leaning against the stall post. "You doing a bit of gardening Rudy?"

Rudy grinned. "Bit of weeding be more precise."

Barrett looked at the other riders. None seemed particularly interested in the conversation. Bakerfield spoke up. "What the hell Red, we gonna make this game or not?"

Barrett nodded. He saluted the old man, and clipped his horse forward. The old man waved as they moved of into the distance.

f_t

A squawk sounded from above. Rudy watched the bird hover. Soon there would be others.

"Easy buzzard," he called out. "Gotta let the desert tame him a little first." He patted the colt who was marking the ground nervously at the presence of the buzzards. "More than a month's money you'll bring my lovely."

He walked behind the wooden wall where Jarak's corpse was slumped. He picked up the rifle he had left on the corpse's chest, giving it an admiring look. He glanced back to the dead man. "Well Injun, your whore gave me this." He took a small medallion out of his pocket and shoved it into the dead man's tunic. "I'll be sure an' tell her how you escaped with your life from the Barrett gang when I come back next week. She'll like that. Might even like it enough to give me a free ride."

A while later Rudy kicked the hard clay off his spade and tied it to his mount. He cantered off, the colt tied behind him. He rode in the direction the six men had come from, away from Bolton town. He weren't much of a card player anyway.

–The End–

D. L. Chance

The son of a Pentecostal minister, Donald L. Chance was born on ancestral homelands in South Carolina and grew up playing music in small churches all over the United States. He went on to a long and satisfying career as a professional musician (specializing in various styles of country and southern rock music) before giving in to another lifelong passion: the written word. Honing his writing skills with fiction was only natural, and led to combining his musical expertise with the journalism of his college days when he was asked to cover country music for his local paper. Dozens of short stories and novels later, along with several thousand news and feature stories for several newspapers, wire services and magazines, Chance is enjoying following in the footsteps of his literary heroes such as Steinbeck, Twain and McMurtry. Currently, Chance is happily juggling careers in both music and writing, and not only has a new album of original songs (on which he played all the instruments himself) available for worldwide download, but a new collection of short stories ready for a summer 2018 release. He and his wife of 40+ years live in North Texas.

Line Shack Winter

D. L. Chance

Charlie Phipps manned a high-country line shack on the Rocker O spread in Wyoming for years. He enjoyed the isolation, the work and the scenery. All in all, there was no place else he'd rather make his meager living. Little did he know, fate had a far different future in store for him.

His job consisted mainly of saddling up one of the stock horses he kept on hand and scouting for strays a couple times a week. When he found enough to make the ride worthwhile, he would haze the wayward cattle back to the summer pastures halfway downslope with the rest of the herd. But if a few were stubborn enough to winter over in the higher altitude, he'd round them up and keep them fed until spring thaw in a large shed not far from the cabin. A fast-flowing creek running beside the shack kept him, his horses and any cattle around the place in plenty of water. And a natural hot springs a pistol-shot distance from the cabin helped round out his personal comforts.

If he got tired of eating beef from the prime steer the foreman let him butcher and smoke for his pantry every year, there was always plenty of other game in the woods along the ridge above the small one-room log house. The same forests provided all the firewood he needed, along with a variety of berries and other wild snacks he thoroughly enjoyed stocking up on when they were in season.

In the evenings, and when it was too snowy to do much outside, he enjoyed playing his guitar and humming the blessed old hymns he'd learned at his dear churchgoing mother's knee. When he was in the right mood, he would sometimes write simple rhyming verse in one of the ledger books he kept on hand for jotting down doings around the cabin that the boss might ask about someday. Some of them were solemn and thoughtful, but most of the poems Charlie wrote came from a deep love of fun and laughter.

He kept the books, and a precious stock of well-used pencils, in a small rough-plank cabinet nailed to the wall directly over his bed, and he guarded them jealously. Any critters looking to get into his meager store of writing supplies—and there were always plenty of squirrels, chipmunks and rats looking to get in and steal some warm winter bedding, especially in the fall—would have to go through him to get at the books and pencils.

Another pastime Charlie enjoyed was throwing his tomahawk. He used to tell how it was given to him directly by Chief Broken Nose, of the Northern Cheyenne, but he had to stop when a real Cheyenne stock wrangler threatened to use it on him if he didn't stop making up silly names and stories about imaginary people. Charlie had never been very accurate with the 'hawk, but scars on most of the trees around the cabin offered silent testimony to the fact that it wasn't because he didn't practice. He kept it hanging on the wall by the same nail that held the bentwood-and-sinew snowshoes he used—along with a furry pair of knee-length Lakota moccasins—to get around the place when the midwinter snows were thigh-high and powdery.

But what Charlie mostly liked about living at the line shack was the seclusion. The endless days of solitude that taught him not to just look at the high country splendor all around—the ever-changing vistas, the interplay of both the wild and domestic animals, the sounds that insisted on being recorded in long stanzas of pleasant poetry—but to become one with it.

And he enjoyed the silence—the peaceful absence of noise, especially the man-made kind that could cascade so relentlessly from the constantly moving mouths of the boys in the bunkhouse.

Here, he could talk to the trees, to the animals, to the hillsides, to the wind, to himself and—except for the wind and some of the animals—they hardly ever talked back. At the headquarters . . . he didn't like thinking about living anywhere near the bunkhouse.

But he did look forward to spending his usual week in town during the summer. It was a thirty-mile ride one way, but with nothing to spend his pay on through the year he always had plenty of jingle in his britches when he rode in. He always rode home broke, but thoroughly satisfied in all the various ways an unattached man of temporary means can possibly enjoy.

One day, when he was getting the place ready for his eighth winter in the line shack, Charlie spotted a rider coming up the valley and recognized him as the ranch hand who worked the line shack in the next valley over. The man was leading two pack mules loaded with winter supplies for both outposts, and he'd probably stay the night before heading to his own place at sunup. Charlie had a big supper of beef stew and cornbread made from the last of his supply of meal hot and ready on the potbelly stove when the man pulled up out front and dismounted.

"Dave," Charlie said, standing in the doorway.

"Charlie."

"Hungry?"

"A mite."

"Fiddle?"

"Always."

They swapped quick nods of the forehead, men of few words who understood each other without a lot of yakking.

While Dave went to take care of his horse and get the pack animals unloaded, fed and put away in the barn for the night, Charlie set the table. Later, they played a few tunes. After running through all the songs they both knew, they stopped playing and just sat staring silently into the fire.

"Changes," Dave finally said, taking a deep breath. "Yep."

"Yep."

"Change is a coming, all right."

"I reckon." Then, blinking, Charlie looked over at the other cowboy. "Wait a minute, what changes? What the hell are you talking about?"

"The foreman is sending his oldest boy up here to winter over with you." Dave shrugged. "He wants the kid to learn how to work a place like this."

"Me?" Charlie set his guitar aside. "Why not send the kid to winter over with you?"

"I reckon it's probably because I told him how you been pining for company," Dave said, a grin playing at the corners of his mouth. "Otherwise, he might be sending the boy over to my place."

"Why the hell did you tell him that?"

"Because I don't want no—"

"Hell, I don't want him here neither!"

"How do you know, Charlie? Hell, you might like having him around."

"You might like having him around, too!"

Dave carefully laid the fiddle beside his chair and reached into his pocket.

"The ramrod said if you balk I was to give you this here note," he said, handing over a folded piece of paper. "He thought you would."

Charlie turned the paper so that he could see it better in the firelight. "Charlie, let the boy stay with you," he read out loud.

He read it through silently a few more times, and then cocked a suspicious eye at Dave.

"You wrote this on the way up here," he said.

Dave held out his palms innocently.

"I won't lie to you, Charlie. I did write it. But it's what the man would have told you if he thought—"

"Nope, I'm not having it!" Charlie wadded up the paper and tossed it into the fire, and immediately regretted it when he realized he could have written something on the clean side of it. "That's just plain cheating, Dave. It's not right."

"Okay!" Dave sat back in his chair, and sighed deeply. "How 'bout we cut cards for it?"

"Gambling's a sin," Charlie pointed out.

"It sure is," Dave said, reaching into his other shirt pocket. "You want to shuffle 'em?"

"Damn right I do!" Charlie laid his guitar over his knees, strings down, and reached for the bedraggled cards. "You think I was just hatched, or something?"

"Not now, I don't," Dave muttered, glancing at the smoldering embers of the phony note and handing the cards over. "But be easy with them. They're all I've got."

"Then let's use mine." Charlie came to his feet and, taking his guitar, crossed to his bed to hang the instrument by its rope strap on the nail where he kept it. Checking to make sure Dave wasn't watching, he opened the cabinet door where he kept his writing materials and found the new deck of cards he'd picked up on his last trip into town. "I can trust these," he said, returning to his chair and handing the cards to Dave. "Cut 'em."

The cowboy took the cards in his work-rough hands and expertly mixed them up, then reached down to set them on the floor.

"Best of three?" he asked.

"What's wrong with one cut?"

"Just making it a little more fair. 'Course now, if you only want one cut, I guess—"

"Best of three, then!"

Dave came up with a four, and Charlie was feeling pretty good about the first cut.

Until he turned up a deuce.

"That's one for me," Dave said, smirking.

"I can count to one, same as you."

"Okay. How 'bout you go next?"

Wordlessly, Charlie turned over a five, and it was his turn to smirk when Dave came up with a trey.

"This 'un tells the story," Charlie said, reaching for the stack again.

He cracked his knuckles and wiped his fingertips on his shirt, and reached deep into the pile. He turned over the queen of clubs,

"Well howdy Ma-am!" He waved the card in Dave's face. "Let's see this feller here try to—" He stopped gloating and his smile disappeared when Dave came up with a suicide king from the cards left on the floor. "I'll be damned."

"Nice deck of cards," Dave said, handing his cards over. "Wanna cut one more time for 'em?"

"No!" Charlie gathered up the cards and dropped them into his shirt pocket. "I reckon I'll need 'em now to keep the kid occupied."

Dave gazed thoughtfully at his old friend for a long moment.

"Look, Charlie, if he gives you too much trouble, you can—"

"Send him over to your place? Good. Why don't you just take him to begin with."

"I never said I'd nursemaid no kid all winter! I was gonna say you can send him back home to his mama if he gets to be too big a handful."

"The boss said I can do that?"

"No, but once he's back at headquarters there won't be much anyone can do about it."

"Except fire me," Charlie pointed out. "The boss can do that."

"He damn sure can."

"Damn."

"Well then," Dave said, reaching for his fiddle, "now that we got that settled, I reckon I'll be moving on come first light."

"Uh-huh. So you won't—"

"You won him fair and square, Charlie."

Defeated, Charlie's shoulders slumped.

"I reckon."

Charlie dropped back onto his chair while Dave, careful with his fiddle, took the other one.

"By the way," Dave said a few silent moments later, "I was told to pass the word along that a rogue grizzly has moved south into this part of the high country. It 'pears to be a big 'un, too."

"How big?"

Dave shrugged. "Couple of the boys down at headquarters thought they saw it when they were clearing the summer pasture last week, but it was gone when they got there. Word from other spreads is that from the sheer amount of carcasses it leaves behind, it's a great big one."

"What kind of carcasses?"

"Cattle, mostly. Some folks claim it's even taken down full-growed buffalo bulls. But it don't eat what it takes. It just kills 'em and chews on 'em a little here and there before it moves on."

"That's bad," Charlie opined. "A thing like that could put a big hurt on a man's profits for the whole year. Any word on the griz heading this way?"

"There ain't no way to know for sure. It's been showing up on both sides of the range—sometimes killing on this side, sometimes killing on the west side—and there's talk about the Cattlemen's Association hiring a professional hunter to go get it. But there's plenty of places in these mountains for it to hide, so I don't 'spect no one'll kill it unless they're mighty lucky."

Charlie agreed, and by mutual unspoken agreement they let the subject drop.

Dave laid out his bedroll near the fire, and they split the last of the beef stew for breakfast. He was saddling up next morning when Charlie jerked a thumb at the pack mules.

"Aren't you taking a load out to your place?" he asked, noting the double pile of supplies laid out on the straw floor. "Surely this kid don't eat that much."

"I got plenty," Dave said. "And if I run short the Anderson spread ain't but a half-day's ride from the house. It's as far for you as head-quarters is, and I can get anything I need there." He led his mount from the barn. "And besides," he said gazing off in the direction of the main ranch house complex, "I suspect the kid can eat more than either of us can imagine, him still a growing boy, and all."

"I 'magine so."

"So long, Charlie."

"Dave."

When the other cowboy was gone, Charlie moved the supplies into the cabin and spent the rest of the day tending to his regular chores—and trying not to think about his impending house guest.

Four days later, it was getting on toward supper time and Charlie was sitting in the privy out back when he heard someone yelling around at the front of the cabin. Damn, he thought, finishing up his personal business and shrugging into his suspenders. Better go get it over with.

"Hey, Old Timer," a mounted teenager said, as soon as Charlie appeared. "Is this the right cabin? Looks kinda rundown. I've been two days getting here, and I sure hope it is. Wandering around in all these trees and mountains has 'bout got me wore down to nothing. Lost a mare on the way up here, too. She skinned out into the woods and I ain't seen her since. May I never see a patch of woods again! How come these shacks have to be so far out in the woods, anyway? Ain't no cows around here nowhere that I can see. Are you . . . Charlie . . . something? Phillips? Are you Charlie Phillips? You look kinda old to be—"

"Who the hell are you, boy?" Charlie looked the kid over. Tall and red-haired, he was dressed cow enough, and he was packing what looked like an old but serviceable Sharps Big Fifty rifle in a saddle boot. Two empty feed sacks spilled over each side of the pommel on his rather ratty stock saddle, and a thick bedroll was tied behind the cantle. But his boyish youth still clung stubbornly to his peach-fuzzed face. "What do you want?"

A puzzled expression came over the teenager's generously freckled features. "I . . . I'm not a boy. I'm coming up on sixteen years old, and that . . . say, are you Phippo? Phlippy? How do you pronounce your name, anyway?"

"Are you the foreman's boy?" Without waiting for an answer, Charlie pointed at the barn. "Get your horse settled in and fed, then get back to the house. There's a few things you need to know if you're going to stay here."

He turned and disappeared into the cabin, leaving the boy muttering about being called boy again.

The kid jabbered all during supper, and he did a lot of complaining about the beef stew even though he managed to finish off two large bowls of it. He rambled on about his pals at school, about school, about his mother's cooking, about how high up might be, about the preacher's personal habits, about how the storekeeper's pretty daughter was probably too stuck up for her own damn good, and he didn't seem to notice that Charlie never spoke the first word.

"Leastways, that's what I think," he finally said before downing a last bite of cornbread. "How 'bout you, Phillips?"

Charlie slid his bowl aside and slowly looked up to meet the kid's eye.

"First thing is, you're going to sleep in the barn until the first good snow," he said. "Then you can spread your bedroll out in here by the fire. You did bring a bedroll?"

"I ain't sleeping in no barn!" The kid hooked a thumb at the corner where Charlie's slept. "There's a perfectly good bed over yonder," he said, "and it looks to be just my size."

"There's not all that much to do around here," Charlie continued as if the kid hadn't spoken. "But what has to be done has to be done right. There'll be ice to break up in the crik', cattle to tend—"

"I tell you I'm not sleeping in any barn," the kid said, coming to his feet. "My pa—"

"Is a long ways off," Charlie pointed out. "Now, your choices are to do it my way around here, or go back to him." He held up a hand when the kid opened his mouth. "Don't bother telling me you can get me fired," he said. "Your pa might be the foreman, but it was the big boss hired me way back. And I never yet give him reason to complain about my work."

The kid clamped his jaw shut and merely glared.

"That's better." Not daring to show how happy he was that the kid bought his tenuous story about being fire-proof, Charlie came to his feet and walked to his bed. He pointed at his cabinet. "See that? You can't ever touch it." He pointed at the guitar. "See that? You can't ever touch it." He pointed at a single-bit axe hanging on a nail near the door. "See that? You can touch it. In fact, starting tomorrow morning, you can take it outside and start splitting that pile of sawed logs up'side the house. But don't ever leave it outside when you ain't swinging it. There'll be more chores as I think of them."

"Is this because I said I wanted your bed?" The kid snorted. "I was only funning you. What's the matter, Old Timer? Got no sense of humor?"

Tempted to spit something equally nasty at the boy, Charlie merely stretched and let go a fake yawn, and pointed at the door.

"I could use some kindling chopped up for the breakfast fire," he said. "Did I mention how the axe is hanging on this nail right here?"

Wordlessly, the kid stalked out.

Charlie was trying to calm his nerves with a few hymns a half hour later when an explosion went off from the direction of the barn.

"Damn!"

He pulled his boots on over his longjohns and grabbed his Winchester on the way out the door. The kid was nowhere in sight, but he could see lamplight peeking through cracks in the barn wall. Otherwise, all was quiet under the bright half-moon.

"What the hell was that?" he barked from outside the building, careful not to go busting in. "What are you shooting at in there?

In a moment, the big door squeaked open and the kid, with the massive Sharps fifty caliber hunting rifle in his hands, looked out and grinned.

"I was cleaning my rifle, and I guess it kinda went off," he said sheepishly. "I'll fix that hole in the roof come morning."

Torn between wanting to yell at the kid for doing something so stupid, and allowing how it was in fact a good idea to keep the heavy gun as clean as possible, Charlie let out the deep breath he'd been holding.

"Why'd you pack along a Sharps Big Fifty?" he asked. "By the time you get it shouldered, whatever is big enough and mean enough to need that kind of firepower to stop will have either already killed you, or bid you good day and run clean over the horizon."

"Oh yeah," the boy said, resting the single-shot rifle butt on top of his bare foot. "That reminds me. My pa told me to tell you there's a big grizzly running loose somewhere in the mountains around here. He said if I saw it a regular Winchester probably wouldn't do more than make it mad, so he made me bring along this Sharps."

Charlie looked from the kid's face to the rifle, then back to the kid's face, then back to the rifle.

"Well, be more careful with it!"

"I will."

Charlie expected the kid to say more. But when he didn't, Charlie turned toward the cabin and went inside to bed.

For the next couple of days, the kid mostly kept his mouth shut and did what he was told. But he gradually started talking more and more until it seemed to Charlie as if the foreman's son couldn't stay awake without yammering away about some damn thing or another.

One evening, as the autumn air grew colder and colder, Charlie allowed the kid to stay longer inside by the fire. Remembering how Dave had said the foreman wanted the boy to learn some cowboying, Charlie took his prized fifty-foot riata down from its special linen-wrapped nail and began rubbing a chunk of beef fat into the tightly braided leather. He'd won several roping contests with it over the years, and he never knew when he might need it. Might show the kid a few tricks with it.

"I've gotta go check that there's good water flow at a tank downslope five miles or so," he said, turning to look at the kid. "It's the only good water hole for better than a half-dozen sections. You can stay here or ride along and see what it takes to keep it running." He tested the suppleness of the lariat, and began wiping it dry with a piece of burlap. "If the windmill quits, there's lots of cattle that could die."

"I'll go," the kid said quickly. "No offense, but this place it getting mighty tedious to look at. A change of scenery might go good."

"At least it'll give you something different to talk about."

The kid looked puzzled. "What?"

He didn't add anything, and Charlie didn't want him to, so they parted for the night and were on the trail leading to the prairie water tank at sunup.

At the tree line, where the open range spread out before them, Charlie pulled up and pointed at the twirling windmill blades visible in the distance.

"There's usually a bunch of wild hogs around there," he said, making sure his Winchester was handy in its saddle boot. "Don't bother 'em. They'll keep their distance while we're working, but they'll attack if they think we're going to hurt their young'uns."

"Why don't we shoot one or two? I love pork. I get so tired of eating beef sometimes. It starts tasting like—"

"When we leave, I'll drop one and we'll take it back to the house," Charlie snapped. "That's what I was gonna tell you if you'd ever shut up." He didn't like the way the riata draped over the rifle butt. "Here," he said, handing over his trusty leather lasso. "Hook this over your saddle horn, and don't—do not—drop it."

"I reckon I know how to handle a lariat."

"Make sure you do."

Charlie briefly wondered if he would come to regret uttering those words, but he tentatively shrugged it off as a case of itchy nerves.

A few squirts of oil from a can in a small tool chest nailed to one of the windmill legs erased a slight squeak in the gear machinery up top. Water was flowing smooth and cold into the small pond at its feet seconds after Charlie pulled the lever that re-engaged the mechanism.

The kid never even stepped to the ground. He passed the time watching the thirty or so hogs milling around fifty feet from the water-hole, and making foolish comments about how tasty they looked.

"We'll get one, don't worry," Charlie said, moving to examine his mare's off hind leg. She limped a couple times on the ride in, and he wanted to make sure her shoes were cleared. "Hold your mud."

With his back to the kid, he didn't see when the boy nudged his own mare forward. Using his knife blade to pry a pebble from the horseshoe, Charlie didn't see the kid shake a large loop in the lariat, either. But

Charlie did turn in time to see the foreman's boy swing the lasso over his head a couple times, then toss it at the herd of wild hogs.

"Damn!"

He was almost in the saddle when a half-grown porker—a boar if its nether region decorations could be believed—stepped in the loop. Before Charlie could get both feet set in the stirrups, the kid pulled the lasso taut on a hind leg and the adolescent hog let out a screech like a train wreck.

Instantly, all the other hogs joined in. They squealed and stomped and kicked up enough dust to hide their brethren on the inside of the herd, and they closed ranks around the smaller pigs.

Both cowponies, not used to dealing with critters that could produce such a racket, shouted their own manic cries. Charlie did his best to rein his mare in, but she wasn't having it. She wanted to get gone, but ended up in the small pond instead. The best he could do was get her started bucking, spinning around and through the muddy, knee-deep water.

When she would swing around just right, he saw that the kid was having similar troubles of his own. But, he saw, instead of simply dropping the riata, the kid had looped the slack end around his saddle horn, and his horse was about to throw him right in among several tons of incensed pork on the hoof.

The kid was game, though. He hung on.

But some of the larger hogs, those battle-hardened old boars with the long tusks made for slashing at bigger animals, were starting to circle around the panicked mare and her equally terrified rider.

And the noise seemed to get louder and louder all the time.

"Drop the rope!" Charlie managed to get some control over his mount, and he cautiously approached closer to the boy. "Drop the damn rope, boy!"

"Don't call me boy!"

"Dammit, I—"

"You said don't drop it!"

"Let the damn rope go, or those hogs are going to eat US!"

"It's too tight! I can't work it loose!"

Charlie pulled the knife he'd used to clear the horseshoe, and moved closer.

"Edge this way and I'll cut it!"

But the kid's mare couldn't be controlled.

Taking a deep breath, and choking on the dust, Charlie spurred his horse forward and deftly parted his beloved old lasso with his knife, then galloped on past the outlying layer of fuming, thoroughly-insulted wild hogs.

Free from the rope, the boy's mare spun around and shot toward the foothills in the distance, dragging at least twenty feet of riata behind her.

Three muscular boars paced Charlie's mount for better than a hundred yards before giving up and turning back to where their kinfolk were still angrily cussing out Charlie and the kid in hog.

He caught up to the boy within another minute or two. Taking up the slack in the ruined lasso, he untied it from the kid's saddle horn and slowly worked it into as neat a coil as he could manage. He took extra time with the five feet of unraveled leather thongs that had dragged the ground.

"Damn."

"Come to think on it some," the kid said, glancing back at the windmill, "I never cared all that much for pork anyway."

They rode along in silence for a long time, until the kid gave a quick snort.

"You gotta admit, though," he said. "That was kinda funny back yonder."

"It weren't funny, and don't you ever say it was again in my hearing!"

The kid shrugged. "I won't," he said. "But it would be funny if you had a sense of humor, Old Ti—"

The look on Charlie's face shut the kid's mouth tight.

Outside of complaining about having to sleep in the barn again, the foreman's son stayed quiet enough for the rest of the day. Heavy storm clouds moved in overnight, and by morning a good foot of snow had fallen. The kid came dragging in as Charlie stood at the potbelly stove frying two large slabs of venison—and wishing it was pork chops—his bedroll, rifle and other personal effects in his hand, and shut the door behind him.

"I ain't sleeping out there no more," he said boldly. "It's too cold."

Charlie pointed at the fireplace. "You can lay out your bedroll at night, but keep it rolled up during the day. And keep your possibles sack out of the way, too. I don't aim to be tripping over your stuff all winter."

The kid did as he was told, and was back at the stove a moment later, rubbing his hands and smacking his lips.

"Sure smells good," he said. "'Course now, bacon would have smelled a lot better than—hey, I'm just funning!"

Charlie dropped the stick of stovewood he'd reached for back into the box and jerked a thumb at the table.

"Sit," he snarled.

"Know what goes good on a night like this?" the boy asked, instead of doing what he was told. "Bear meat. I had some here 'while back. It was sorta greasy, but I've heard it can be fixed so that don't matter none. Ever eat bear meat?"

"No."

"I have," the kid said, a note of superiority in his tone. "If that big grizzly comes anywhere 'round here, I think I'll just butcher him and smoke him. Bear meat goes good on a night like this."

"Sit down," Charlie growled.

"I'm down." The boy eased into a chair and sat fidgeting while Charlie put a pot of coffee on to boil. "Sure wish I'd thought to bring along some paper and a few pencils," he finally said. "It's gonna be a long winter without 'em."

"What do you know about paper and such?" Charlie asked suspiciously, turning from the stove and carefully keeping his eyes from straying to his private cabinet. "Why do you want 'em?"

The kid shrugged. "I like to draw is all. When it snows heavy, a little drawing makes the time pass by quicker. The days don't seem so dreary and dull."

Charlie moved the deer meat to a pair of tin plates, along with the coffee and a pan of stovetop biscuits he'd cooked before turning in the night before, and set them on the table.

"I got cards," he said, taking a seat across the table from the boy. "Does your ma let you play much poker?"

"Poker?" Reaching for his share of the food, the kid shrugged. "Not much," he said, his voice taking on an unusually even tone. "So I haven't had all that much time to get any good at it. Besides, I don't have anything to play for. Um . . . you?"

His fork stopped halfway to his mouth, Charlie studied the kid's eyes for a long, silent moment. Then, laying the bite back on his plate without eating it, his own eyes narrowed into an angry frown.

"I told you to stay out of there," he said softly. "I catch anything messed with, and you're heading back to your mama today. Today. Now."

"I didn't mess with nothing," the kid said. "I just happened to glance in there once looking for some . . . matches. But I didn't see any, so I shut it back."

"Now why the blue hell would I keep matches clear across the cabin from the stove?"

"I . . . okay. I was just curious. But I didn't touch anything."

Obviously not believing the boy, Charlie snorted and went back to eating.

"But if you don't mind teaching me to play poker, I wouldn't mind learning." The kid chewed a bite of deer meat and gazed wistfully off into the distance. "I'd think I could learn a lot about it from someone who has played as long as you."

"You got nothing to bet," Charlie snapped, irritated at himself for showing too much interest in the proposal. "It wouldn't be worth my time."

"I've got my time," the kid said. "If you were to bet, say, a piece of paper and the loan of a pencil against, say, an hour of me not talking out loud, maybe we could—"

"You'd bet your silence?"

"It's all I've got." He met Charlie's steady stare with one of his own. "If you don't care for conversation, that is."

Thinking that at no time had there ever been any such thing as an actual two-sided conversation between them since the boy arrived, Charlie took another bite and chewed thoughtfully.

Three monotonous snowy days later, as the kid happily added shading touches to a mountain scene he had going in one of Charlie's books, Charlie sat in his chair by the fireplace and strummed his guitar as loud as he dared without breaking strings, trying to get louder than the kid's incessant description of what might be on the mountain he was drawing. Finishing a song he particularly liked, ordinarily, he pulled the new deck of cards from his shirt pocket and tossed them into the fire.

That night, the winter boredom ended when the door was smashed to splinters.

Instantly, Charlie was on his feet, his Winchester in his hands.

"It's that grizzly!" he yelled, pegging a couple shots through the open doorway while the kid cowered, screaming in his bedroll. "You've got the Big Fifty, boy! Shoot it!"

"I—I don't know where it is!"

"It's—" Charlie looked away from the door for an instant and spotted the big rifle leaning against the far corner of the room. "Why the hell did you leave it over yonder?" he cried, jerking his eyes back to the door in time to see the massive bear's snout appear.

By the time he levered three more rounds through the Winchester, the bear, screeching in agony from at least two hits, had his whole massive head and neck inside.

The giant hairy nightmare's shoulders looked too wide for the opening, but Charlie knew it wouldn't be long before the monster worked his way inside, and could finish him and the kid off at his leisure.

"Get over yonder and grab that gun, boy!" Charlie shouted, blasting another two shells at the bear. "This one ain't even slowing him down!"

"Don't call me boy!"

"Dammit, boy! I—" The grizzly turned pain-maddened eyes on Charlie and screamed one last enraged yelp at him before jerking backwards out the door. "Go get it now!" Charlie cried at the kid.

The kid ran to the corner and hefted up the big rifle, but it dropped from his shaking hands, firing off a round that roared angrily past Charlie's left ear when it hit the floor.

Charlie ducked, and glanced up to see the heavy bullet had hit his guitar right where the neck joined the body, breaking it into two large pieces and hundreds of smaller ones. He groaned inwardly, but turned away from the destruction to yell at the boy some more.

And he saw the bear's head appear in the doorway again.

"Damn!"

He shouldered the Winchester, but the grizzly ducked away before he could fire.

"Get that rifle loaded!" he screeched at the kid. "Ain't no telling when that thing'll be back!"

"I can't," the kid said, tears appearing in his eyes. "I only had two shells for it, and they're both gone now."

"Two . . . two?"

"Pa said they're too expensive, and one should take down just about anything."

Charlie closed his eyes and thought a minute. "Okay," he said, "under my bed yonder is an old Henry Yellowboy. And a box of shells, dammit! Go get it and load a full—"

From outside, he heard a commotion that sounded like more wood being broken up, then he heard horses and mules screaming in terror.

"It's got into the barn!"

Charlie took a minute to pull on his clothing—he had to order the kid to do the same—and shrugged into his heavy coat. He thumbed enough rounds into the Winchester to top it off again, and dropped the rest of the box into his coat pocket. There was no way to darken the cabin without dousing the fire, so Charlie carefully approached the door and peered off toward the barn, where the bear was still knocking things over and making plenty of racket.

"Either the animals are all dead, or some got out okay and are gone," he opined softly to the boy. "We won't know until that big sumbitch leaves. If it does. You got that Yellowboy loaded?"

The kid nodded.

"Okay, I'm going to . . . hmmm."

"To what?"

Charlie gazed toward the far corner. In a hole dug under the floor, he had two sticks of dynamite. He brought up a half dozen sticks several years ago to enlarge the hot springs behind the house, and he still had those two left over.

His Winchester might not kill the grizzly quick enough to do him and the kid any good, but a well-placed stick of dynamite or two might do the job nicely.

"Go get me that axe, then watch the door," he said, walking over and stomping on the floorboards.

When he was sure he had the dynamite located, he had it out within a minute, to the kid's surprise.

"You had them things under there? What if the Sharps had shot through the floor instead?"

71

"Then the grizzly might be dead by now," Charlie said, taking a piece of stove kindling to the fireplace and holding the end of it in the flames. "Of course, so would we."

Clearly terrified, the boy nodded at the dynamite. "What do you aim to do with them?" he asked, an obvious tremble in his voice.

"I aim to kill that damn bear," Charlie said. "And I aim to do it now. Keep me covered from here with that Yellowboy, and empty it into the grizzly if this here dynamite don't work."

Cautiously peeking around the ruined door jamb again, Charlie caught a glimpse of the grizzly in the barn door. The burning stick of kindling in his left hand, and the two sticks of dynamite in his right, he boldly stepped through the door.

"Hey you big bastard! Come and get me!"

The grizzly bellowed long and loud, and charged.

Charlie was surprised at how fast something so big could run through snow deeper than its legs were long, but it was halfway to the cabin before the short fuse on the first dynamite stick was sputtering fully to life. Sweat gathering on his nose, Charlie drew a deep breath and watched the fuse. He knew that throwing the dynamite too soon would be just as deadly as throwing it too late, and he only had one chance to get it right.

It seemed as if the bear was right on top of him when he tossed the dynamite a few feet out in front of him and backed quickly into the house, bashing into the kid on his way in.

He pulled the boy to the right and, his back to the log wall, clapped his hands over his ears. The explosion rocked the cabin and belched an enormous cloud of smoke and snow through the door.

Instantly, Charlie shouldered his Winchester and took careful aim at the door. But when the smoke cleared, he heard the bear's wheezing roar receding into the woods in front of the cabin.

Stepping gingerly out the front door, he spotted the huge dark shape limping quickly down the slope, and it wasn't long before he lost it in the darkness. But while he could see it, he thought he could make out a smoke trail behind it.

"Is it . . . is it gone?"

"I doubt it," Charlie said, suddenly looking around inside the cabin for the second stick of dynamite he no longer held, but didn't recall dropping. "It's hurt, though, and that'll make it want some revenge, or I don't know grizzlies."

"Known many grizzlies, have you?"

"Not many. Just this one." Charlie spotted the dynamite near his bed—a safe distance from the fireplace. "And that's aplenty."

He plucked another few pieces of kindling from the stove box and tossed them into the fireplace. When they flared up enough, he added more firewood, and then drew a burning stick from the tiny inferno.

"I'm going down to the barn to look around," he said picking up the dynamite and dropping it in his coat pocket. "You stay here, and if you see anything of that bear again, fire off a couple rounds. Don't let it walk up behind me, understand?"

The kid's face turned strangely white in the firelight, but he nodded anyway and held the Yellowboy even tighter.

At the barn, he saw that one of the mules was mutilated pretty thoroughly and left torn into two roughly equal halves. But apparently its pack partner and all the horses had gotten away clean.

And they weren't likely to come back for a long time.

On the way out, he nearly tripped over the tackroom door. The grizzly must have pulled it of its hinges and . . . yep. Charlie eased the firewood torch into the storage room and saw that the bear had clawed the saddles to shreds, and chewed what was left of his adored riata to slimy leather strings.

But the thick, four-plank slab door seemed to be solid. The original cabin door, it had a horizontal gun port cut in the center two planks for when proddy Cheyenne war parties roamed these mountains and plains. He hefted up the door and, dropping the torch into the snow, dragged it toward the house.

He was nearly there when the kid started firing.

Charlie looked to his left and saw the massive shape of the grizzly coming quickly up the slope again.

He dropped the door.

"Bring me some burning wood!" he cried, pulling the second stick of dynamite from his coat pocket. "Now, dammit!"

A burning torch in his hand, the kid met him at the door, and Charlie held the flame close to the fuse.

Instead of coming straight at the house, the bear angled toward the barn. While the boy disappeared some damn where, Charlie stood ready to light the fuse the instant the bear decided to charge the cabin.

Warily, the bear entered the barn and emerged momentarily with what Charlie could see was the back half of the dead mule in its mouth.

"Well ain't you bold as you please," Charlie muttered. "Waltzing right in here again like that mule is personal property you accidentally forgot!"

Growling and snorting, the grizzly dragged the carcass down the slope and out of sight, leaving a dark smear of mule blood in the snow.

Charlie let go the breath he didn't know he was holding, and eased the dynamite back into his pocket.

"Come stand guard," he said over his shoulder. "I'm gonna get this other door up."

The door was installed within an hour and the cabin was warm and cozy again. While the kid moaned and muttered and sometimes cried out in a restless sleep, Charlie kept the fire going and, his Winchester and the dynamite nearby, a close watch on the door. He was pretty sure he heard sniffing around the door a couple of times, but if it was the bear coming back it didn't try to get in again. By the time he could see the grayish light of what must be at least mid-morning through the rifle port on the door, Charlie knew what he had to do.

He had to go out in the snow, afoot, and kill the grizzly once and for all.

On hearing about the decision, the kid dropped to his bedroll and looked like he wanted to cry.

"You're just going to leave me here? B—By myself?"

"I got no choice." Charlie made sure the Winchester was topped off with a full load of 44.40, and that he had plenty of matches for the stick of dynamite he had left. He intended to leave it with the kid at first, but then he remembered what happened with the Big Fifty rifle—and why it wasn't available to him now when he needed it the most. No sense in letting the kid blow up the cabin while he was gone. "I can't bring you along because I can't watch out for the both of us at the same time. And besides, you got no winter duds. You'll freeze out yonder before the day is out." Sitting in his chair, he tied the snowshoes on over his furry moccasins and thought about what else he should tell the kid without overburdening the boy's terrified mind with too much information.

"So keep the fire going all the time," he finally added, "and have that Yellowboy in your hands every minute."

Charlie peered through the rifle port before pulling the door open, just in case the grizzly was still nearby. He didn't see any fresh sign, but he did notice a newer trail of mostly covered-over paw prints leading downslope in the direction the grizzly dragged the mule carcass last night.

"When I leave," he said, turning back to the boy, "brace this door shut with the Sharps. There's nothing in here heavy enough to hold it if that bear comes back, and the Big Fifty is the only thing strong enough."

A tear slipped from the kid's eye. "How do I brace it?" he asked, gesturing at the floor. "There's nothing to stop it with."

Charlie studied the situation for moment.

"After I'm gone, take the axe and cut out small notches in the door and the floorboards," he said. "But make damn sure you measure it first. If the door opens even a little bit, the gun will fall out of place and leave you with nothing."

"O—Okay."

With nothing else he could think of keeping him—and he desperately tried to think of anything that could delay his having to walk out, alone, into the winter in search of a wounded, murderous grizzly bear—Charlie pulled the door open and stepped outside. Then, on a whim, he reached back in and pulled his tomahawk from its nail beside the opening.

"Might need to cut some firewood," he muttered, sliding it handle-first into his belt. "Better than nothing."

Without looking back, he pulled on his work gloves and trudged out into the snow, ignoring the axe-on-wood noise that started up in the cabin behind him.

At a hundred yards downhill, out of direct sight from the cabin, he saw where several sets of old tracks made the same abrupt turn to the south—to his right—and he realized the bear was even wilier than he first gave it credit for.

"So that's the way you wanna play it," he muttered, unslinging his Winchester and levering a round into the chamber, just in case. "Okay. You can deal this hand, but then it's my turn."

Instead of following the tracks, he crossed the frozen creek and moved parallel with them for a good quarter of a mile before he lost sight of the tracks in a thick tangle of hemlock trees. He had his rifle raised to fire a probing round or two into the thicket when a sudden flurry of birds leaving their perches a few hundred yards to his right caught his attention. He glanced over and caught a quick glimpse of dark fur disappearing around the shoulder of a small rise.

"Leading me further away from the house, are you?" he murmured softly. "Don't think I don't know what you're up to."

He cautiously approached the rise from a different direction, where he picked up the bear's tracks there again.

Charlie followed the tracks until an even colder nip in the air reminded him it was getting on toward an early evening. He was too far from the cabin to risk heading back in the dark, so he looked around for a tree he could climb. He knew the smaller black bears could climb trees, but they should all be asleep in their winter caves by this time of year. He had no idea if a half-ton mountain of determined grizzly meat and burned fur could climb as well, but he didn't think it was possible.

A massive cottonwood tree growing alongside another frozen creek looked like something he could climb. With a thick deadfall limb as a kind of ladder to help him get started, Charlie shoved the points of the snowshoes down the back of his coat and climbed into the cottonwood. He was breathing heavily when he reached a three-limb junction about twenty feet from the snow, but he dared not settle for a perch any lower.

Charlie used his tomahawk to clear away a few branches so that he could wedge himself more or less comfortably among the three thick limbs, with his chest to the trunk so that at least his front could stay warmer than it would with his back to the tree. And besides, he reasoned, if the bear came back and shook the tree, his arms would be in a better position for him to hang on for his life. Settled in, he checked to make sure the dynamite still lay safely in his coat pocket before he pulled a thick chunk of last summer's beef jerky from the other pocket. With the food inside him, he knew he could eat snow to quench his thirst without worrying that it would rob him of precious life-giving inner heat.

Sometime later, he slept.

He was startled awake by noises on the ground several times in the endless night, but it was always deer or other critters that belonged there. Once it was when a bull moose rubbed its antlers against the tree trunk, and he came awake twice to the sound of wolves trying to get up the trunk to his roost.

Sunshine in his face woke him early the next morning, and, cold, stiff and sore, he gazed around. He didn't see any animals of any kind waiting for him at the bottom of the tree, and there were no grizzly tracks in sight.

Scanning the distance, he just could make out a fairly fresh line of familiar-looking tracks ascending to the top of a bald ridge, then disappearing over the hill about a quarter-mile to the south. The bear had stayed somewhere close during the night before moving on sometime after the snow stopped falling, he realized.

Looking all around, he didn't see any tracks showing that the grizzly had returned. He pulled another piece of jerky from his pocket and chewed on it awhile for breakfast while thinking over this turn of events.

If, as it appeared, the monster was moving on south to bother someone else—and their annoying house guests—Charlie decided it was a waste of his time and effort to follow it. After all, he'd fought it off the best he could, and maybe that was good enough. Maybe it learned not to mess with him, or his dynamite.

"Let's just hope so, at least," he said around a bite of dried beef. He swallowed the last bit of jerky before easing down a few limbs toward the ground. The deadfall limb he'd propped against the cottonwood trunk was no longer where he'd placed it, so he took one long last look around before tying on his snowshoes and committing himself to dropping to the snow. "Get it over with," he muttered.

On his feet, he made sure the Winchester was ready to fire, just in case, and started back toward the cabin.

As he trudged through the snow, thick clouds moved in. Before long the forest was misty with a frosty fog that eventually crusted his face over with a light coating of ice. And he couldn't see as far through the trees.

Every once in a while he would stop and listen, his rifle shouldered and ready to fire, at little noises he heard in the woods. But when he didn't see any movement, he'd cuss himself for a scared fool and keep going.

Charlie wasn't sure just when he became aware of it, but sometime in the mid-afternoon he began to suspect that—even though he hadn't seen any bear tracks heading back in—instead of the hunter, he might have become the prey. About an hour later, a flock of birds suddenly taking to the air fifty yards or so behind him and to his left caught his full attention.

He picked up his pace, moving as fast as he could in the cumbersome snowshoes. But it was still slow going.

The cabin was in sight when he crossed the last frozen creek. He hadn't gone more than a hundred steps beyond it when he heard the now more-than-familiar bellow of the big grizzly behind him.

Laying his Winchester on the snow, he reached into his pocket for the dynamite and a light—but he couldn't get a match going with the gloves on. As carefully as he could, he pulled off his gloves and moved backwards, desperately trying to light the stick of instant death. But nothing he did could coax the match to life.

The bear emerged from a thicket across the creek and bawled long and loud at him.

Without a piece of rough steel to light the match . . .

Charlie recalled the tomahawk in his belt. He jerked it out and dragged the match across the slightly rusty steel blade and, to his surprise, the match caught fire and held.

Moving slowly and deliberately, the grizzly started shuffling toward Charlie. He could see that large patches of its fur were singed, and some of the hair was missing in spots.

He had to hold both the dynamite and the 'hawk handle in his right hand, but he finally got the fuse to sputter to life. Just as he started to throw the explosive death, his right snowshoe caught on something and he stumbled and nearly fell backwards.

Charlie dropped the dynamite!

Without thinking, he snatched it up in his left hand and lobbed it underhanded in the direction of the bear. But it dropped back into the snow less than halfway to the deadly animal, where the fuse apparently sputtered out.

Crossing the creek, the grizzly roared again and stood on its hind legs, getting ready for a final charge.

Charlie came to his feet and, forgetting his Winchester where it lay, began running toward the cabin as fast as he could in the snowshoes.

"Open up, boy!" He dragged as much air into his lungs as possible, but they were beginning to burn quicker than he ever thought they would. "It's on my heels! Open the damn door and start shooting at it!"

He glanced back to see how close the bear was, and he saw it break through the ice and fall into the stream—but it was up and on its feet and screaming again, even before Charlie could turn back to watch where he was going.

He was within yards of the cabin door when he heard the grizzly chuffing up behind him.

"Open the damn door, boy! Open it!"

Charlie hit the door with a force that caused icicles to break off the eaves, but it stayed tightly shut.

"Dammit, open the door and shoot at this damn bear!"

He turned to see the grizzly charging the last few yards toward him, then he noticed he still had the tomahawk in his frozen right hand. Closing his eyes tight, he flung the old Indian war hatchet in the direction of the roaring bear before sliding on down to sit in the snow at the bottom of the door.

With an ear-torturing shriek, the grizzly leaped the last few feet . . . and fell stone dead with its giant head landing heavily in Charlie's lap.

Charlie opened one eye, and almost poked the tomahawk handle into it.

He drew a deep breath and levered both eyes open to find the tomahawk blade almost completely buried in the bear's skull.

Charlie fell over backwards when the kid jerked the door open. With the bear pinning his lower body to the ground, all he could do was lay stretched out halfway inside the cabin. He looked into the unbelieving face of the kid—who held the useless Sharps Big Fifty instead of the Yellowboy in his hands—and drew a deep breath.

"Okay, boy, here it is," he sighed. "I killed it, you clean it."

His guitar and cards gone, Charlie spent the rest of the winter letting the kid teach him how to draw while he taught the kid how to write decent rhyming verse; and he was almost—almost but not all the way—sorry to see him ride out with the spring thaw.

But occasionally over the next few years, he couldn't help wondering why the kid didn't think he had a sense of humor.

–The End–

C. F. Eckhardt

His full name was Charles Frederick but he used his initials because his name was too long to get on one line. He went by Charley with an 'ey' because he wasn't a perfume. He was born in Austin, Texas, and grew up in an atmosphere where Texas and Southern history were part of his life almost from the day he was born. The man across the street was born when Texas was still a republic, the man next door was the grandson of one of Jim Bowie's companions at the Calf Creek fight in 1831, the man up the street was visited frequently by an elderly uncle who knew way too much about a couple of Clay County, Missouri, boys named Dingus and Frank than any peace-loving feller had any business knowing, and just down the creek lived a feller named J. Frank Dobie.

Eckhardt grew up in Austin and on about 400 acres of hardpan, cedar brake, and honeycomb limestone in western Williamson County, Texas. He attended the University of Texas where he majored in history and held a BA in the subject. Since jobs in 'the history bidness' were hard to come by unless one was politically 'correct'—which Eckhardt spent a lifetime refusing to be—he spent many years as a peace officer and soldier. Finally tiring of being a moving target, he pursued a trade that would allow him both the time and the intellectual energy to pursue his first love, writing about Texas and the American West.

Eckhardt's books included *The Lost San Saba Mines, Unsolved Texas Mysteries, Texas Tales Your Teacher Never Told You, Tales of Bad Men, Bad Women, and Bad Places, Four Centuries of Texas Outlawry,* and *Texas Smoke—Muzzle-Loaders on the Frontier,* illustrated by Wesley G. Williams

Charley passed away in the early hours of May 18, 2015, at the age of 75, following a brief illness.

Coming Home

C. F. Eckhardt

He hurt. He hurt bad. He knew the slug missed the bone—otherwise he wouldn't have been able to mount. The blood hadn't spurted, so it also missed the artery. It didn't come out in a flood, so it hadn't hit a major vein, either, but he was still bleeding badly. The bandanna he tied around his leg was soaked in blood. He had to find some help somewhere or he'd bleed to death and Simon Lawton would have succeeded.

Simon Lawton didn't do his own killing, he hired it done. The gun he hired to do the job was dead. The man got off the first shot, but it was his only one. A load of buckshot caught him square in the chest, right between the nipples. At twenty feet, even a sawed-off shotgun doesn't spread much.

He finally saw a house as the big buckskin gelding rounded a turn in the road. He headed for it, riding at a slow walk. It had been almost three hours since the shots were exchanged and it was possible the wounds were forming scabs. He didn't want the jarring of a trot to break them loose. As he reined up in the sand-covered yard he called out. Almost immediately the door opened. A woman stepped out—a nice-looking woman, too. He judged her to be about thirty.

The only thing that didn't look good about her was the double-barreled shotgun she had leveled on him. "What do you want?" she demanded. Her voice was not friendly.

"Is your man around, ma'am? I been hurt purty bad an' I ain't sure I can get outa this saddle on my own."

"I got no man," she said. "How'd you get hurt?"

"Well," he said, "a feller tried to kill me, but he didn't quite do it."

"You've been shot? Where?"

"Right leg. Been the left 'un, I wouldn't never a made it into the saddle. Don't know if I can get off by myself. That's how come I asked 'bout your man."

She put the shotgun down and came to him. "I'll help you down," she said.

"I'm a right big feller, ma'am," he said. "Heft might near a hunderd an' ninety. You sure you could do it? You ain't all that big."

"I'm a strong woman, mister. You just slide out of that saddle real easy an' I'll get you in the house." He eased out of the saddle, dragging his wounded leg over the high-dished cantle. The pain made him gasp. When his right foot hit the ground the leg started to crumple. The woman got on his right side where he wore his pistol in a crossdraw. She supported him as she guided him toward the steps.

"Better lay me out on the porch, ma'am," he said. "I'd be liable to soak your beddin' with blood, I get on your bed."

"I'll get you into the kitchen, lay you out on the kitchen floor. I can boil some water, get you cleaned up, get a proper bandage on your leg. Why did a man shoot you? You aren't on the run, are you?"

"I'm on the run in a manner a speakin', ma'am, but not from the law. Feller as put this hole in my leg, he was paid to pull the trigger. Man as paid him, he don't do his own killin'. Leastways, he don't do it no more. 'Twas a time he did, but he's mighty high-falutin' these days."

"Why would he pay someone to kill you?" she asked.

"To keep me from killin' him. It goes back a ways, ma'am. Nothin' to trouble you 'bout."

She put him on the clean kitchen floor. With a pair of scissors she cut the right leg off his brown ducking trousers, then off his drawers, then split both so she wouldn't have to pull his boot off. "It looks to be a clean wound," she said. "Dark blood. Not from an artery. I'll have to clean the blood off, get a proper bandage on it." She drew water from the inside pump and poured a cup, then handed it to him. He drank greedily. It had been hours since he had water. She got out some huck toweling, cut it into two pieces, then tore a strip off the long side. Then she took a small bottle from the cabinet. "This will hurt," she said.

"What is it?"

"Iodine. It's all I have, but it'll help keep the wound from festering." She applied the dark-red substance to the holes. He gritted his teeth and gasped at the touch. It was almost as if she'd set his wounds afire. Then she folded the two sections of huck into pads, positioned one on each side of his leg, and tied them in place with the strip. "Can you stand?" she asked.

"Apt to need a mite of a hand gettin' up, ma'am," he said. "'At right leg, it's mighty feeble right now." Getting behind him, she lifted his shoulders. He grasped the edge of the table and managed to pull himself to his feet.

"You're southern," she said. "I can tell by the way you talk."

"Yes'm. Georgia. Dahlonega County."

"Were you in the War?"

"Yes'm. I was with Johnston, fightin' Sherman. I was jus' a button kid then—sixteen, but I lied 'bout my age. I was at Kenesaw Mountain, but I got wounded a couple days later so I got left at a farmhouse outa Sherman's path. By the time I healed up the War was over. Went back home, but there warn't much to go home to no more. Sherman's bummers found it. Folks got clear, but they burnt the house an' barns, burnt Paw's corn in the field, kilt our ol' cow an' the hogs. Butchered the hogs an' carted 'em off. Emptied the smokehouse an' then burnt it down, too."

"My husband was in the Eighth Ohio Infantry," she said. "He lost an arm at Cold Harbor. He was just a boy, too—nineteen. He came home. I was just seventeen, he was twenty-eight, when we married. We came west to homestead in Nebraska, but we picked the wrong part of Nebraska. We came down here to New Mexico, to the mountains. We bought this place from a widow. Her husband got killed in Lincoln County in seventy-nine."

"Ridin' with the Kid or agin him?" he asked.

"Neither. He was just in the wrong place at the wrong time. When the shooting started there was no place to go. He was just crossing the street, she said, when all of a sudden the air was full of bullets and one hit him in the heart. Let's get that gunbelt off you and get you on the bed."

"Reckon I better keep my shooter where I can get at it, ma'am, jus' in case 'at feller what shot me has some friends. You better put my horse outa sight, too. Anybody comes lookin' fer a feller with a bullet in him, you ain't seen one. Don't wanta kill nobody in your house, but I don't wanta get kilt here, neither. They get me, they'll hafta kill you, too. You'd be a witness."

"What's your name, mister?" she asked.

"Ben Scarbrough, ma'am. An' yourn?"

"Alice Bickford. My husband was Robert Bickford. I lost him an' both of our babies to cholera last year." Her voice was strained. "It's hard to think about it, even now. It was a Saturday—town day. It hit them about ten in the morning, on the way to town. Why it passed me by I don't know, but it did. All three of them were dead by one that afternoon. When I got the wagon to town, cholera was all over the place. It lasted about five days and then it was gone, but it killed my family and about thirty other people—nearly a quarter of all the people in town."

"Mister Scarbrough, who wants to have you killed?"

"Feller name of Simon Lawton."

"Simon Lawton? The man who owns the Elkhorn Saloon?"

"That's him."

"But why would a successful man like Simon Lawton want you dead?"

"Like I said, to keep me from killin' him."

"Why would you want to kill him?"

"Goes back a ways. I had a sister. Purty gal she was, too. Real belle a' Dahlonega County. He's from Dahlonega County, too. He commenced to sparkin' my sister. She let him know right off she didn't want no part a him. He figgered he couldn't have her, nobody could. He kilt my sister. Shot 'er down right on the porch of our new house. I was there. Didn't have a gun on me, so I couldn't shoot him. He was sittin' on his horse when he shot her. Then he lit a shuck. Got clean outa Georgia. I been trackin' him nigh on ten years now. Got a Georgia murder warrant in my saddle pockets. Got a Dahlonega County deputy sheriff badge in there with it. If he'd go peaceable I'd take him back to Dahlonega County to hang—but he ain't goin' peaceable.

84

"He's got power an' money now, too. I was to go to law, he'd buy 'em off. He done that in Miss'sippi, first time I run him down. He ain't buyin' off no law this time, an' he ain't gonna buy me off. Ain't 'nuff money in New Mexico to buy me off. Marybelle's been in 'at grave near on ten year now. I aim to put him in one."

"You're going to have trouble. He's in with the government here. It goes all the way to Santa Fe. They may hang you for killing him," she said.

"'Long's he's dead first, don't matter what happens to me. Marybelle's killer'll be six foot under. That's all I care 'bout."

f_t

His wound healed slowly but, fortunately, cleanly. He stayed at Alice Bickford's house, sleeping in the washroom in his soogans. As soon as he could, he began to do chores for her—chopping wood for the stove, feeding the animals. He took her rifle into the woods and brought back a fat white-tailed deer and a couple of hogs that had no earmarks. They salted the venison and smoked the pork. He helped her in her vegetable garden, digging potatoes and onions out of the soft soil, cutting and shelling the peas for her to put up.

Fall became winter and they huddled together in the house next to the kitchen stove, trying to keep warm as the snow fell. And slowly but surely, they fell in love. The kisses were passionate—but there was nothing more.

"No, Alice," he said. "I ain't leavin' you with a baby in your belly an' no man to go with it. After I finish what I got to do, if I'm still 'live I'll put a weddin' ring on your hand. Then we can think 'bout babies."

Come spring his wound was fully healed. He saddled the buckskin, hung the shotgun on its thong from the saddle horn. "You come back to me, Ben Scarbrough," she said.

"I finally got something to come back for. If I live, I'll come back to you, Alice." He put spurs to the buckskin and rode away at a trot.

Midday, he walked into the Elkhorn Saloon. "Lookin' for Mister Simon Lawton," he said.

"What you want with Mister Lawton?" the barkeep asked.

"I'm an old friend," he said. "We growed up together."

'Oh. I'll tell him." The barkeep headed into the office. Ben Scarbrough stepped behind one of the pillars that held the roof up. He loosened his six-shooter in the leather.

Simon Lawton came into the room. He was wearing striped pants, a blue, watered-silk vest, a fine linen shirt. He had a gold watch chain across his vest. He was smoking a cigar.

"Where's this so-called 'old friend?'"

Ben stepped out from behind the pillar. "Right here, Simon," he said.

"Ben Scarbrough! I thought you was dead!"

"You tried hard 'nough to make sure I was. It's over, Simon. I'm either gonna take you back to Dahlonega County to hang, or one of us is gonna die right here. It's your choice, Simon. You're gonna be dead either way—or both of us will be."

Simon Lawton reached for his hip pocket—he kept a Colt Lightning, a short-barreled sheriff's model, in a leather holster there. Ben's left hand flew to the crossdraw holster. The forty-five spoke once and a bright red spot appeared just above Simon Lawton's vest. His hand kept moving and the Lightning came out, but he never fired it as he crumpled to the floor.

"Somebody get the law!" the barkeep yelled. "He's jus' murdered Mister Lawton!"

"Fair fight ain't no murder," one of the customers said. "Lawton reached first. I seen it. How come you kilt him, mister?"

"I'm a Dahlonega County lawman an' I got a murder warrant with his name on it in my pocket."

A deputy, following the sound of the shot, burst through the swinging doors from the cigar apartment into the saloon proper. "What happened here?" he demanded.

"I'm a Dahlonega County, Georgia, deputy. I got a murder warrant with Simon Lawton's name on it in my pocket. I told him I come to get him, take him back to Dahlonega County to hang, or we could finish it right here. He went for a gun." Ben reached into the inside pocket of his vest and produced a document.

"You're a ways from home, mister. What's your name?" the deputy asked.

"Ben Scarbrough."

"Says Lawton was wanted for killin' a Marybelle Scarbrough. Any kin to you?"

"My sister. He shot her down 'cause she told him she wouldn't marry him if he was the last man in the world."

"You say he went for a gun." He turned to the saloon's customers. "Anybody else see him go for a gun?" Several responded that they did. "Well, that makes it self defense, any way you look at it. Sheriff's gonna wanta talk to you, Scarbrough, but I don't reckon we'll do anything else. Was I you, I'd watch my back trail, though. Lawton's got some friends."

"I know he does," Ben said. "He hired one of 'em to kill me last fall."

"What happened to him?"

"He run head-on into a load a buckshot. If Lawton didn't collect his carcass the wolves got him. Need to wire the Dahlonega County sheriff's office, tell 'em the warrant's been served."

"Who's the sheriff there?" the deputy asked.

"Hell, I don't even know. I been on this trail nigh on ten years. Ain't set foot in Dahlonega County since I took it up."

At dusk, Ben pulled rein in front of the Bickford house and dismounted.

"Alice," he called. "I'm back."

She came out the door and looked him over. "At least you don't have another hole in you," she said.

"Near thing, but I got him. Marybelle can rest easy now."

"I can rest easy now, too," she said. "Welcome home, Ben." She ran into his arms.

–The End–

John T. Biggs

Don't bother trying to classify John T. Biggs' stories. They are a genre stew of speculative fiction, anthropology, mystery, and humor written in a mainstream literary style. Native Americans play a significant role in most of John's narratives. He reworks traditional Indian legends and sets them in modern times, the way oral historians always intended.

Sixty of John's short stories have been published in magazines and anthologies that vary from literary to young adult speculative fiction and everything in between. Some of these stories have won regional and national awards including Grand Prize in the Writers Digest 80th annual competition, third prize in the Lorian Hemingway short story contest, and a Storyteller Magazine's Peoples Choice Award.

John has published four novels: *Owl Dreams, Popsicle Styx* (Oklahoma Book Award Finalist) *Cherokee Ice* (Oklahoma Book Award Finalist & OWFI Best Published Fiction Book of 2015), and Shiners (OWFI Best Published Fiction Book of 2017), as well as a linked short story collection, *Sacred Alarm Clock*, which includes the OWFI Crème de la Crème winning story, "Twenty Percent Off."

The best way to see what John is up to is on Twitter: https://twitter.com/biggspirit or his Amazon Author Page: www.amazon.com/-/e/B00GW5A1QU

Sky Stone

by John T. Biggs

Bird Singer didn't like anything about peyote, the bitter taste, the way it made the moon twist across the night sky, and especially the nausea. He tried not to think about it while he chewed dried cactus buttons. Waiting was the hardest part of a vision quest; a holy man needed patience.

"Help me." His prayer was weak, but so was his magic. Rain callers could make demands of the spirits, but a shaman like Bird Singer had to beg for visions like a camp dog at the cooking fire.

"Please help me."

Coyotes sang to him from across the desert. Whether that was a good sign or bad remained to be seen. He released a pinch of corn pollen into the air and grasped the amulet bag he wore around his neck. Most of his helping spirits didn't fly at night, but he called on them anyway. Lives hung in the balance.

A coyote bit a woman three days ago. Would a killing spirit fill her mouth with foam? Would sickness spread through the pueblo? He needed answers.

The wind nudged Bird Singer along a path through stray boulders and jojoba plants, just as she'd done on the day his spirit helper chose him—the proudest day of his life, when he brought the red-backed hawk down from the sky with a single pebble from his sling.

Bird Singer moved where the wind pushed him until he came to a solitary set of Hopi sandal prints. What fool would travel alone at night? His eyes followed the gentle curve of the trail until he found the answer.

I am the fool. Tricked into a circle. Peyote's laughter filled the air, like music from an abalone shell wind chime. Then the melody stopped, replaced by harsh Apache words and more coyote songs.

Were the marauders and the tricksters laying traps? With spirits, nothing was certain.

"Help me."

A yellow light flashed in the western sky and five red streaks reached toward the world. A dust cloud rose where the nearest bright finger touched the desert. Now Bird Singer knew where Peyote intended him to go, but he was in no hurry.

f_t

The Apache lay face down between a smoldering fire and a blanket. Bird Singer hid in the brush and weighed the possibilities. No breathing motions, but Apaches were famous for deception.

The shaman held his breath until he couldn't hold it any longer. He held it three more times. Even an Apache warrior couldn't go so long without breathing.

Bird Singer moved on all fours, like big cat stalking a rabbit. He knew little about Apaches, but he knew this: the raiders seldom traveled alone, and they never ventured far from camp after sunset. There was only one explanation for this solitary warrior. The dead man was a shaman, like Bird Singer. He'd been seeking supernatural wisdom when the spirits struck him down.

The items on the dead man's blanket confirmed Bird Singer's suspicion—a falcon's wing, a copper bell, and two perfectly round rocks with mineral patterns that made them resemble human eyes. The contents of the holy man's medicine bundle were laid out to attract helping spirits. The fist-size hole in his back was evidence the magic didn't work.

Bird Singer rolled the holy man over so his eyes were open to the sky. He removed an eagle feather from his amulet bag and brushed it first across his own lips, then across the dead man's.

"The sacred lands don't welcome you," he said. "Carry this message to your brothers."

Death's touch had made a hole straight through the Apache, and left a depression in the sand filled to the top with blood.

Like a ceremonial cup, an offering to the living desert. Did it hold anything else? A power object Bird Singer could add to his amulet bag? The Hopi shaman plunged his arm into the warm dark liquid, staining his tunic sleeve to the elbow.

His hand closed on the spirit gift. He lifted it from the pool of blood and rolled in his hand; a lump of shining metal with a surface like a glistening collection of bubbles. Heavier than stone and warm to the touch.

Peyote whispered, "Spider Woman's gift."

Bird Singer closed his eyes and chanted a prayer for guidance. When he opened them, he saw the silhouettes of three large dogs at the top of a nearby hill. After a dozen heartbeats, an Apache warrior joined the dogs—then another, and another.

One of the warriors shouted a command and the animals charged.

How did Spider Woman mean for a Hopi holy man stop three war dogs? There had to be a way. The gods didn't bestow gifts on a man one moment and kill him in the next.

The dead man's medicine bundle. The two eye stones on the Apache holy man's blanket were the perfect size for Bird Singer's sling. He loaded one stone at a time and sent them flying.

Two solid cracks, like a cottonwood limb breaking under the weight of ice. Two of the three charging animals fell to the ground with fissures in their skulls large enough to free their souls. The third dog skidded to a stop. He might have run away but the warriors on the hilltop urged him on.

No more eye stones on the blanket. The falcon's wing and copper bell were useless.

The sky stone. Would Spider Woman strike him dead for using it? The dog would surely kill him if he didn't.

"Forgive me!" He loaded the sky stone into his sling and sent it flying. Bird Singer followed the path of the power object in the moonlight. The silver talisman pierced the throat of the charging animal in a gush of blood.

The Apache warriors moved cautiously down the hill. They'd watched him dispatch three battle-hardened dogs with a weapon favored by children.

As the men approached, Bird Singer drew a deep breath and made his owl call. He knew the night birds carried souls to the land of the dead. He hoped Apaches knew that too. Three more calls in quick succession, then he clutched his amulet bag and waited for the magic.

Four perfect calls brought the Apaches to a stop but they didn't break and run until a great horned owl flew out of the darkness and perched on the dead man's chest.

Bird Singer ran as well, and while he ran, he sang a song of thanks to Spider Woman.

f_t

"Where is this power object?" Six elders ruled Bird Singer's pueblo. Each one asked him the same question. This time the interrogator was old lady Larkspur, matriarch of the Ant Clan.

"Why didn't Spider Woman give her gift to a rain maker?"

Bird Singer tried to plead his case without sounding argumentative. "The spirits toss. The shaman catches."

Old lady Larkspur wasn't convinced. Bird Singer used a power object to kill a dog, not the stuff of legends.

"What of the coyote?" Five elders already asked that question, but that didn't stop the matriarch from asking it again. "And the woman who was bitten?"

In the end, they believed enough to send scouts looking for Apache raiders. They posted sentries and planned ceremonies.

As old lady Larkspur put it, "The spirits favor those who take precautions."

f_t

Several days passed with no signs of the raiders. There were rumors of Ute warriors attacking a Tewa pueblo twelve days walk to the north; perhaps Bird Singer had seen stragglers from that battle.

"Or perhaps," one of the elders suggested, "Peyote played a trick on the shaman."

Even Bird Singer began to have his doubts. He'd gone into the

92

desert seeking a coyote vision; perhaps the trickster filled his mind with nonsense.

The shaman purified his body in a sweat lodge, denied himself food and water, and prayed for guidance from the creatures of the air. He sat cross-legged in the plaza focusing his mind on the pristine spirit of the red-backed hawk, when a vulture fluttered from the sky and landed at his side.

Bird Singer opened his eyes and watched the vulture pace around him. "Welcome, Bird Who Cleans The World. What news have you brought me?" The vulture made four circles around the shaman, each one larger than the last. People gathered in the plaza to watch the vulture do what vultures never did.

"The bird has been poisoned!" suggested an old man. It was possible. Alkali salts covered low-lying regions of the desert. Rivulets of water ran through them and collected in poison pools. Perhaps an animal drank from one of these pools, died, and was eaten by this vulture.

"Look!" a young girl shouted, "The bird's foot prints make a power spiral."

The vulture's path formed the familiar twisted pattern the Hopi used to decorate their pots, the same pattern in which corn and beans were planted. No one doubted this vulture was a spirit messenger.

The carrion eater stopped pacing, hopped over to Bird Singer, and regurgitated the contents of its stomach directly in front of him. It made a slow, graceful turn, tested its wings and ran to the south, the direction of good news. The Bird Who Cleans the World launched itself into the air and rode the wind over the horizon.

Something silver glittered among clumps of dog fur, deteriorated muscle, and strands of intestine. The shaman reached into the partially digested remains and retrieved the sky stone. He held it up so that everyone around him could see. Now they would have to believe him.

ft

Discussions of the spirit visitation buzzed in every household. People spoke in whispers whenever the holy man approached. The story of the vulture and the sky stone took on the features of a legend. The problem was, no one knew how the story would end.

No one had seen anything like the sky stone. Its glittering surface exceeded the brightest gloss a skilled artisan could produce on the richest nugget of native copper. Some of the older villagers had seen polished discs of gold carried by traders from the distant south, but even those treasures hadn't sparkled like Spider Woman's gift.

"There is nothing to fear," the shaman promised, but old lady Larkspur told him to keep the talisman out of sight.

"It has killed an Apache holy man and a war dog," she said. "Then traveled in the belly of a carrion eater." No one could imagine what kind of power the sky stone held.

"It killed an enemy of the Peaceful People," he told the old woman. "It fell from the heavens. It was lost and then returned by a creature of the sky."

The Shaman placed the sky stone into his amulet bag. At least the people believed in Bird Singer's Apaches, even if the scouts found nothing.

"The spirits took me to the enemy once before," Bird Singer told the elders. "Perhaps they'll do it again."

But the War Chief refused his company.

"A man might be in the spirits' favor one moment, and broken out in boils the next. My men won't walk beside a wizard."

The shaman didn't like the sound of that. It was a small step from wizardry to witchcraft. When things went wrong, people went looking for a witch. If the rain failed to come, if the corn failed to grow, if a sickness swept the pueblo, a witch could find himself buried in a shallow grave with a large stone pinning his soul under the earth. When he heard people refer to the Apaches as "the shaman's spirit enemies" he knew it was time to act.

ƒt

The night sky was familiar but not friendly. The quarter moon provided barely adequate light, and shooting stars flew across the heavens at a rate of one or two in every hundred heartbeats.

Bird Singer comforted himself with mental chants to keep the forces of the world in balance. His life would find its center again once the Apaches were discovered. The coyotes would regain their fear of people. Bird Singer could resume his place as a lesser shaman whose principal function was persuading eagles to give up their feathers.

A cloud of bats fluttered across the moon. The tiny creatures consorted with spirits of the sky after the sun had set, but in the daylight hours they hid in caves. Bats concealed themselves almost as well as Apache raiders.

Could that be a message? Caves were good for hiding bats and Apaches.

Perhaps the night fliers would help a holy man who could speak with owls. Bird Singer removed the sky stone from his amulet bag and held it in his hand. He rolled the sky stone through his fingers, appreciated its complex cobbled surface in the moonlight, offered a prayer of gratitude, then tossed it high into the air.

A large bat dove and caught it.

Chief of the bat tribe.

When bats are fooled into snatching tossed stones, they drop them quickly, but the Bat Chief didn't do this. He carried the sky stone high above his tribe. The talisman glittered in the moonlight like a star, and when the bat released the power object, it fell so slowly that Bird Singer caught it easily in his extended hand.

"Thank you brother."

The dark flyers made a slow turn in front of the crescent moon. They fluttered across the night sky in a swirling motion easy to follow from the ground. The shaman fell behind, but moonlight glittered on the creatures' wings like sparks carried on a gentle breeze.

By the time he lost sight of his spirit guides, the holy man could hear the voices of Apache warriors. He crouched, still holding the sky stone. The raiders had chosen their cave wisely. Its mouth opened onto an empty part of the sacred land. Cracks in the rock carried smoke from their fire through a thousand tiny chimneys where it wouldn't be seen even in the full light of day.

Twenty warriors sat around a smoldering fire, boasting, laughing, and pulling chunks of meat from a charred leg of venison. Hopi archers could make short work of this lot. Bird Singer held the talisman in his open hand and offered a prayer of thanks.

The sky stone was a dazzling gift. It concentrated the intensity of ambient light while holding the distorted images of the stars and moon on its cobbled surface. Bird Singer watched the entire night sky roll around his palm. The reflected light pulsed and flashed in cadence with his prayer. The effect pulled at his mind the way trickling water draws a restless spirit into sleep. For a handful of heartbeats he forgot about Apaches.

Then the light dimmed. It had been weeks since the Rain Callers had been about their business and the sky was completely clear. It was not a cloud that obscured the illumination of the stars and moon. The shaman rolled the stone a little more, and a face reflected from its surface, an Apache face.

Without breaking the rhythm of his prayer, Bird Singer found a rock almost too large to hold in his free hand. He stood, turned and threw the stone in a single movement without stopping to aim.

Masau, the god of life and death, was the shaman's ally that night. His rock struck a large Apache warrior squarely in the forehead. The man went down without a sound.

Only one!

Bird Singer felt the warrior's chest, no heartbeat. He heard the Apache's soul escape with his final breath. The shaman looked back into the cave. Two dogs stood in the entrance, taking in his scent. They bared their teeth, put back their ears. It wouldn't take the warriors long to notice.

There were plenty of stones on this mountainside. Bird Singer found two suitable for his sling. In less than ten beats of a frightened heart, the dogs fell dead at the mouth of the cave.

Before the animals stopped twitching, the shaman mimicked the sound of the great horned owl—four calls, quickly followed by another four. The effect on the raiders was immediate.

Bird Singer recognized a few words: witch, demon, evil spirit. He made four more owl calls, tucked Spider Woman's gift into his amulet bag, then broke into an easy run.

Only after his breath grew ragged did he risk a look behind him.

One lone warrior walked toward him from the direction of the cave. One more than he anticipated.

Bird Singer picked up his pace as much as the uneven terrain and the darkness would allow. He expected the warrior to give up the chase and return to the safety of his cave, but the man's silhouette remained a constant feature on the mountain landscape. The warrior plodded across the desert carrying neither bow nor lance. He meant to tear the life away from the Hopi shaman with his bare hands. Or worse, he'd capture Bird Singer, take him to his band's main encampment and give him to their women.

ft

The sun peeked over the edge of the world as Bird Singer reached his valley. Only half a morning's run to his pueblo if the Apache didn't kill him.

When Bird Singer looked back over his shoulder one last time, the warrior broke into a full sprint, closing the distance between them with every pace.

The shaman clasped his amulet bag and prayed as he ran. Only the spirits could save him. The holy man's heart raced like a sparrow hawk's. His muscles burned and tightened enough to double him over. His chest ached. The rush of blood through his ears sounded like the ghosts of his ancestors calling him to the afterlife.

Bird Singer stopped running. He turned to face his death.

The Apache warrior slowed his pace, no longer in a hurry to finish things.

The shaman would either escape or die this day; he would not be taken alive. He opened his amulet bag and removed the sky stone. The talisman had saved him twice before. Perhaps it would save him again.

"Power is with me!" Bird Singer looked to the heavens and chanted, holding the sky stone in the open palm of his left hand. "My need is great."

His adversary stood twenty paces away. He'd drawn an obsidian stiletto and assumed a fighting stance, but his eyes were not turned toward the shaman.

A large male coyote moved from the shadow of a boulder and fixed his attention on the Apache. Foam dripped from the animal's muzzle; it staggered as it moved toward the warrior. If this was the same animal that attacked the woman from Bird Singer's pueblo, evil days lay ahead of her. The bite of such a creature would turn a human into a monster.

No one deserved such a death, not even an Apache marauder.

The warrior stepped backward, matching the coyote pace for pace. He knew the demon would own his body, even if he killed the animal it possessed. He held his stiletto ready and prepared to meet his doom.

The coyote stumbled as he tried to leap—once, twice, three times. Bird Singer drew his sling. He loaded the weapon with the sky stone, and by the time the animal sprang, his missile was in the air.

The silver talisman flashed in the morning sun like a lightning bolt as it struck the coyote's head. The animal fell at the warrior's feet. It trembled for a moment, and then lay still.

The Apache knelt beside the coyote. He reached out to touch the animal that had almost taken his life, but his hand changed course before his fingers brushed against the creature's fur. Instead he grasped the glittering object that lay beside the dead predator.

The warrior stood holding Bird Singer's talisman in his outstretched hand. There was no malice in his eyes as he approached the shaman.

The Apache spoke a single word when he placed the sky stone into Bird Singer's hand. He said the word again as he walked away.

The holy man returned Spider Woman's gift to his amulet bag. He understood almost nothing of the Apache language. But he understood this: his people would have no trouble with these raiders.

–The End–

Big Jim Williams

Big Jim's latest novel, *Jake Silverhorn's Revenge*, set in Frontier Arizona, follows his successful Cattle Drive book, the Western Fiction-eers' Peacemaker 2014 Award Winner for Best First Novel. Audio books are, *The Old West*, and author/narrator, *Tall Tales of The Old West*. Anthologies credits include, *Best of the West, Sundown Western Tales* (Sundown Press); *Dead or Alive, Broken Promises* (La Frontera Press); Western Fictioneers' *Wolf Creek* books, and, online or print magazines, *Frontier Tales, Rope and Wire, Western Horseman, The Cardroom Poker News, Livestock* (Texas) *Weekly, American West, Sniplits, Shoot!*; non-Westerns in *Over My Dead Body, Orchard Press Mysteries, Suspense Magazine*, and the print anthologies, *The Killer Wore Chanberry,* volumes 3 & 4 (Untreed Read Press). *In Vino Veritas* (Horrified Press), *The Last Man* (Sword & Saga), *Murder to Mil-Spec* (Wilmont), and At Home & Abroad (Joyous). His Civil War radio drama, "Close Encounters of the Confederate Kind," a San Francisco *Shoestring Radio Theatre* production, aired on over 100 NPR stations. Williams, a California resident, is a lifelong broadcaster, and retired publicist. His favorites things are dogs, friends, writing, movies, reading, book stores, the Old West, naps, cold beer, buffets, laughing, trying to stay healthy, avoiding trouble, letting others pick up the check, and trying to finish writing another Western novel.

They're Gonna Hang Durango

by Big Jim Williams

When you've been riding days on end, you're sore, damn sore. And every part of the body says . . . enough.

That's how Clay Perrin felt.

Mesquite, his young horse, was tired, too. But the big sorrel was blessed with strong legs, and stamina.

Four days in the saddle, hurrying back to an old haunt was about all Clay's body could stand. "But I gotta get there, or they're gonna hang Durango!" Clay muttered through dry, cracked lips.

When Durango's letter arrived, Clay knew he had to go. You don't forget an old friend when he asks for help.

Clay and Durango were old friends, a kinship that began when they served together in uniform on the dusty border with Mexico. Patrolling the hot desert during the day, and squeezing some life out of a dirty border town at night, wasn't much of a life for two lonely U.S. soldiers. It went on for two years. You don't forget times like that.

Clay hunched lower in the saddle, trying to hide from the chilling night wind. A short Mexican cigar was clenched between his teeth, its glow and smoke provided some comfort. His gloved hand pulled the bulky sheepskin coat tighter around his neck and shoulders.

Those were the days, he thought.

His mind escaped the cold, remembering a time when two young troopers were in one scrape or another. Sometimes fighting with Sergeant Royal. Other times with muleskinners, or deadly smugglers that plied their trade along the Rio Grande River, dividing Texas and Mexico, or filled the dusty adobe towns.

Once it was a fight over one of Spanish Lil's girls. Other times it was a fight with Lil, or one of her girls. Clay smiled . . . remembering. He rubbed the small scar on his chin. The drunken teamster had only hit him once. It's amazing what a broken beer bottle can do. But Durango had been there, kicking the legs from under the big, wild-eyed man, dropping his head on a bar rail.

But that was only one of the times Durango had saved Clay.

Sergeant Royal taught Durango and Clay how to use dynamite, then "volunteered" the two soldiers for a special job. Under cover of darkness, they destroyed a bridge and remote adobe miles below the U.S.-Mexico border . . . an illegal crossing and shoot out that never appeared in any official U. S. Army report. Using guns and dynamite they stopped a band of Mexican outlaws from further border raids into Texas.

During the gun battle, one of the bandits hurled back one of the long sticks of dynamite Clay had tossed into their hideout. Clay froze. The short fuse sizzled at his feet. Durango grabbed the dynamite and tossed it back . . . exploding inside the adobe.

Without Durango, Clay would be dead. But he had learned a lot about dynamite from Sergeant Royal and Durango.

Now Durango needed his help. Clay hadn't hesitated to let the Lazy A's foreman know he had to leave, to help an old friend. That's why he was riding a tired horse on an unfamiliar mountain trail at night. Clay gave Mesquite his head and trusted to luck.

"Hell, he knows more about what he's doing than I do," said Clay, breaking the midnight silence.

He tried to slump deeper into the saddle. He was stiff and tired. He wanted to stop and spread his blankets on the ground under some trees, build a fire, get warm, and sleep.

The cork came easily from the small bottle Clay slipped from his coat pocket. The first burn of the whiskey made him cough; the second swallow brought some warmth to his body.

"That's better," he said. He carefully slipped the half pint back into the saddlebag, between a coil of blasting primer and two small, long bundles. "Gotta keep moving," he said. "Gotta keep moving."

Durango's letter had been short, penciled on yellow paper. Scrawled words reminded Clay of a child trying to tell the world its problems.

"Clay, come help me," wrote Durango. "I'm in jail in Fort Henry. I did not do what they said I did. I'm gonna be hung, Saturday, at sunup."

Other than Durango's name at the bottom of the paper, that's all the letter had said. And if Clay didn't get to Fort Henry by Saturday, it would be too late. Clay knew that. But there were still several miles to go.

The horse continued its slow movement; its flared nostrils exhaled rhythmic bursts of steam. Clay could see snow-capped peaks in the distance, and felt the biting wind cut through his heavy Jacket. He untied his old Army blanket from the back of his saddle and pulled it around his head and shoulders. He leaned forward, his chin resting on his chest. Eventually he dozed in the hard saddle. He drifted in and out of memories and dreams of warm beds, blazing fireplaces, steaming cups of coffee, and platters of hot food.

Later, Clay awoke, and rubbed his eyes, straining to see. He thought he could see a light or two blinking far ahead in the darkness.

"I hope that's Fort Henry down there," he said, softly, patting his horse's neck. "Gotta be . . . unless I'm lost. If it ain't the old Fort, Durango's done for, for sure."

Clay returned to an uneasy sleep, the stub of a dead cigar wedged in the corner of his mouth. He leaned across the pommel, his chin bobbing on his chest, his mind in an uneasy twilight. It wasn't real sleep, but it was something.

He awakened to shades of pale light gently spreading across the desert below, gradually increasing in intensity, silhouetting low mountains circling the long valley holding Fort Henry.

Ahead was the last of the mountain trail. The remainder was steep.

"This looks good," said Clay. He dismounted at a large outcropping of rocks before the trail descended rapidly in a series of switchbacks to the flat desert. He unwrapped one of the packages from his saddlebag, and removed several red sticks of dynamite. He dug a hole with his hunting knife under a large boulder at the edge of the trail. Then carefully placed the explosives, covering them with a thin layer of dirt and pine needles.

"Just might need these later," he said.

He removed an extra canteen and small canvas bag from the rear of his saddle and walked back up the trail, noting a small canyon off to his left. He stopped at two large pine trees, and swung behind the larger of the two.

He returned without the objects, led his horse to the bottom of the steep slope, and stopped on the other side of a dry creek. He glanced up at the outcropping of rocks and surrounding big trees, locked the image firmly in his mind, and remounted. Damn, he was hungry. Should have brought more food, he thought. He searched his coat pockets, found a forgotten strip of dried beef, broke off a piece and stuck in his mouth. He let it soften and sucked the juice. It tasted good. Munching on dry, teeth-cracking jerky in the saddle would do for now. He'd eat at Fort Henry.

Clay left the creek and joined a rutted road. He turned his horse toward several twisting pillars of smoke rising above the old Fort. There was light now. The morning sun felt good on his face. Five minutes later Clay wearily moved into the small cluster of old buildings that hugged the Fort and called itself a town.

Fort Henry . . . stuck in the middle of nowhere . . . wasn't much. More a stockade than Fort with its outer walls constructed of large vertical timbers, logs dragged from the distant mountains. Towers dominated each corner. A heavy wooden gate opened to the west. Long abandoned . . . the old Army Fort now held only a trading post. A small town had grown around the Fort: two saloons, a general store, small hotel, blacksmith, livery, Sheriff's office, and assorted lean-tos.

The Fort's one-room jail survived. Not a real jail, more like a small dungeon; dirt floor and two small barred windows near the ceiling. Durango must be there, thought Clay. He and Durango had "guested" there once after busting up some chairs and a cowboy's jaw in a saloon.

If they're gonna hang Durango, Clay knew they'd probably do it on the cross arm spanning the Fort's main gate. Once, he and Durango had watched the Cavalry hang a deserter convicted of raping a girl from a wagon train. The young soldier had died hard . . . crying and begging for mercy. Clay was sure it would again be the execution spot.

The smell of someone's early morning coffee inside the Fort made Clay hungry for a cup: hot and black. The hotter the better to thaw his hands and warm his insides. He thought hard about going after a cup, but decided to wait until he circled the Fort.

In the old cemetery behind the Fort, someone was digging a grave. Clay didn't like that. The sight of it made him sweat in the morning chill.

"Gotta help Durango," he muttered. "Gotta help."

Clay stayed back from the corner of the Fort where Durango's cell would be, deep under one of the old guard towers. He gave a quick look, but couldn't see Durango peering through the high barred street-side window. Even a condemned man needed sleep.

Not many people were on Fort Henry's street this early, but maybe enough to get curious about a stranger riding in. Clay didn't need that.

Clay thought a lot of strangers would probably be riding in to watch the hanging. Hangings weren't that common any more. And here on the plains most people would welcome any kind of excitement.

By the time Clay circled the Fort a gray morning light began touching the land. An old wagon with a handful of blanketed Indians was approaching the Fort's entrance. Clay tied his horse to an outside hitching rail in the rays of the morning sun. Mesquite would like that.

He stomped his cold feet to renew circulation, and followed the Indian's creaking wagon inside the decaying Fort.

Clay sought out the smell of the coffee. It drifted from a large tin pot bubbling on the back of a red-hot stove in the Fort's trading post.

The coffee sent its warmth through Clay's gloved hands when the bearded man behind the counter offered him a tin cup.

"God, that's good." Clay nodded thanks to the storekeeper, a small man with slicked-down hair and missing left ear. The steaming black liquid spread new life through Clay, helping soothe his saddle-stiff body.

"You're up and about early, young fella." The words came from a smelly fur trapper warming his calloused hands in front of the potbellied stove. He wore a dirty leather shirt and pants, a buffalo coat and Indian moccasins. A long rifle rested across his knees.

"You here for the hangin'?" asked the trapper. "A lot of people is."

"Hanging? What hanging?" asked Clay, acting unconcerned. He avoided the man's eyes.

The trapper tapped his clay pipe on the edge of the stove, dumping ashes on the dirt floor.

"The drifter in the Fort's cellar-jail," he said.

"Oh," said Clay. His hat brim shadowed his eyes. His turned-up coat collar covered both sides of his face. He wanted to avoid possible recognition from years back when he and Durango were Fort cellmates.

"Sunup tomorrow they'll be doin' it," revealed a second trapper, with a picket-fence smile and wind-cutting nose. He squatted in a rickety chair on the other side of the stove, a wad of tobacco squirreled in his cheek. "Hear'd he got in a fight in the Red Grizzly and shot somebody."

"Killed that no-account, Turk Donley, from Colonel Overstreet's spread," said the one-eared merchant, his bony elbows on the counter. "Colonel don't take kindly to nobody killing his men . . . even if they's drunk and festerin' for a fight."

"Guess that drifter took him on," said the first trapper.

"Nobody'll miss Turk," said the storekeeper. His right index finger probed his nose. "Mean and liquored up most of the time. But you don't go shootin' people in Fort Henry—least not one of Overstreet's men."

"Who they gonna hang?" asked Clay, still trying to be nonchalant.

"Some dumb-ass drifter," shrugged the storekeeper. "Should-a skedaddled when Turk pulled his big knife."

The first trapper rubbed sweat from his face with a dirty sleeve. It was getting hot and smoky in the store.

Clay finished his coffee. He casually fingered a stack of shirts, but listened intently to the talk. He bought a blue shirt with large pockets, and a supply of small Mexican cigars. He liked the brand, although they burned too fast. But, with what he was planning to help Durango, fast-burning cigars would be useful.

The stove huggers said Colonel Overstreet had been judge, jury and prosecutor, deciding that Durango—a stranger—must die!

"A tough man?" questioned Clay.

"Overstreet runs this valley . . . and its law, too," said the storekeeper, wiping the counter with his sleeve. "If he don't like you, you'd better buy a ticket on the next stage . . . or a plot in the cemetery."

The three men didn't smile, but admitted they were looking forward to the hanging.

Clay accepted more coffee when the pot was waved in his direction. He moved back from the stove and pale window light. He leaned against a stack of boxes.

"Lots of people in town," said the delighted merchant. "Saloons brung in women, too," he winked.

"Them girls will be busier than fleas on a dog," laughed the first trapper.

"Ain't never seed a hangin' before," said his tobacco-chewing friend.

"Ain't slept with a woman since tradin' for a squaw on the Missouri," sighed the first trapper.

The man behind the counter rubbed his grimy hands together. "Fort Henry ain't had a hangin' since the Army left," he said. Then he grinned, adding: "Business should be good."

Several other men and the blanket-wrapped Indians from the wagon were filling the cluttered trading post. The light from the morning sun stalked across the log walls and floor as Clay slipped out the door. He wandered inside the Fort, and noted the buildings, doorways, alleys, and stables, helpful information in an escape.

The entrance to the jail was unguarded. A big padlock and steel rod held the thick wooden door leading to the musty underground room where Clay and Durango had been held years before. Thirteen planked stairs dropped to a cramped room that was the Fort's old jail. Little light came from two ceiling-high barred windows. One narrow slit opened on the Fort's parade ground; the other faced the town's powdery street and few businesses. Locked up for four days, it hadn't taken Clay and Durango long to memorize what little could be seen.

Fortunately for Clay, Durango had a sense of humor. He enlivened their stay by preparing elaborate imaginary dinners compared to their actual slop-bucket meals. Durango held cockroach races, named the competitors, rewarded the winners with bits of food, losers with the heel of his boot.

Clay didn't know why Durango had returned to Fort Henry. He hadn't said in his letter—a letter that was a cry for help.

Clay hoped Durango could see him from his cell. Would know he hadn't been deserted. That maybe . . . just maybe . . . Clay could help.

Clay wanted to yell:

"Hey, Durango. It's Clay. Don't worry."

But he couldn't risk it. Somehow he'd find a way to let Durango know he was there.

Clay moved across the Fort's small parade ground, his eyes—casually as possible—further exploring the old buildings, stables and corrals, and the narrow, sagging catwalks circling the inner wall. Towers, long abandoned, jutted from the Fort's four corners. Clay had climbed them and the catwalks before.

Less than twenty-four hours wasn't much time to save an old friend from the hangman. Clay had to try! He had a seed of a plan . . . but was too tired to think now.

f_t

It was mid-morning when two men stood in the back of a small field wagon stopped below the long crossbar of the Fort's open gate.

Both wore badges.

The first man was tall and thin, a gravel voice came from his Adam's-apple throat. A full mustache covered his lip.

His squat baggy-pants companion balanced a coiled rope on his shoulder. He cut a plug of tobacco, and stuffed a chunk into his chinless mouth and began chewing under a sagging face and watery eyes.

A small group of rowdies, sharing a bottle of whiskey, provided an audience.

The tall man with the gravel voice took the rope from his short companion, thumbed his greasy hat onto the back of his head, and studied the crossbar.

"It'll do," he said.

Then he slipped his thumbs over his belt, and added:

"Colonel Overstreet told me, 'McCarthy, you're our best deputy with a rope. I want you to hang that bastard that killed Turk.'"

His short companion nodded.

"So, I'm a-doin' it," said McCarthy, carefully forming a noose.

"Damned right!" agreed his chinless sidekick, spitting tobacco juice. "I say drop that noose over that drifter's neck and send him air-dancin' to hell!"

"And I got the rope that'll do it!" shouted McCarthy, waving the completed noose.

The rowdies laughed.

"Turk was a good ol' boy," said McCarthy. He tossed the coiled rope over the overhead beam.

"The best," agreed one of the drunken loafers. He raised a bottle, "Ol' Turk was the best," he repeated.

McCarthy yanked the rope from the beam, and easily repeated the toss several times.

His expanding audience added grunts of approval and encouragement.

Clay watched from along the Fort's inside wall.

He remembered what the trading post man had said: "Overstreet runs this valley . . . and its law, too."

Clay squatted on a blanket in the sun. His lean, tired back rested against his saddlebag and the Fort's logs . . . stiff legs thrust forward. His muscles still ached. He pulled his wide-brimmed hat over his eyes, and folded his arms across his chest and thick coat. A dead cigar drooped from the corner of his mouth. He tossed it on the ground, closed his eyes, and slept.

It was late morning when Clay awoke to the clatter of more horses, wagons, and people entering the Fort. Talk indicated many were Overstreet's men, or from small cattle ranches. A few women with thin-faced kids spread picnic baskets on wagon tailgates. Clay could smell fried chicken and pies. Children played while adults gathered in small talkative groups, frequently glancing toward the underground jail.

Many of the valley's hired hands would soon be belly-high in the town's saloons, or sizing up the sporting gals.

A few men nearby laughed and swapped bets on how long it would take Durango to stop kicking at the end of the hangman's rope.

"This ain't no damned carnival," muttered Clay, his anger growing. "A good man is about to die and you're laughing," he said.

Two small boys and a large black dog stared at Clay. They stood at the end of his outstretched legs, trying to peer under his tilted hat. One boy, with a long stick, poked at the cowboy's boots.

Clay didn't move.

The boy poked again . . . harder.

Clay still didn't move.

Then the kid jabbed harder at Clay's boots.

Suddenly Clay sat up, arms wide, and growled. The boys yelled and ran, regrouping, wide-eyed behind a woman's long skirt. She scolded the boys. Then her weathered face smiled at Clay.

Clay tossed each boy a small coin.

"See, he's a nice man," said the woman, hugging the boys.

A smile covered Clay's stubbled face, and then quickly faded. His legs and body remained stiff. A hot bath and a good meal would help.

He led Mesquite to the only livery stable left in Fort Henry. The tired and hungry horse got the last stall.

Clay talked with the stable owner about buying a second horse, something young and fast. He'd pick one out later. "Need it for someone coming to the hanging," Clay said, casually. "He'll be heading into the mountains, later."

He draped his heavy saddlebags over his shoulder, patted Mesquite, and walked up the street. He dodged wagons and horsemen . . . more arrivals for the hanging.

Yes, there was one second-floor room left, said the hotel's bald manager, and Clay could get a bath at the barbershop next door. Business was good, he said, but he frowned at being interrupted while eating a plate of beans and bacon.

Clay shoved his saddlebags under his sagging hotel bed before returning to the rutted street, busy with more dust, wagons, horses, and people.

The hot bath, shave and clean shirt made him feel better, followed by a big platter of steak and eggs, biscuits and coffee.

Clay reentered the Fort where men were now laughing and shouting insults at Durango, who peered wide-eyed from the slit that served as a cell window. A fat guard with a badge blocked the cellar entrance, waving a shotgun at the boisterous crowd.

"Stay back," he said, enjoying his authority.

Clay remembered being at that same window, pulling up for fresh air, and the limited view. The unventilated cell had smelled of damp earth, sweat, rat droppings and human waste.

Several men, fortified with "bottle" courage, were taunting Durango. Clay joined them. He wanted Durango to know he was there. He yelled too, pushing his hat back with his left index finger, a recognition signal he and Durango had often used.

Durango's sunken eyes scanned the crowd from his ground-level window, and then settled with relieved recognition on Clay's face. The skin around Durango's eyes crinkled, the only sign of a smile he allowed. Then his head quickly disappeared.

Now all Clay had to do was find a way to help his old friend. He was developing an escape plan that would require split-second timing. But if it failed, Clay would either be shot . . . or hanged alongside Durango!

Other than that, thought Clay . . . escape shouldn't be a problem.

ft

By mid-afternoon Clay was seated on a ledge in a deep gully behind the town.

He withdrew two of his new cigars. Using the back of his knife blade he gently marked each several times—in equal segments—carefully avoiding breaking the tobacco wrapper. He lighted one and puffed, then placed it on a flat rock at his side. He lighted a second cigar and did the same, glancing between his pocket watch and the two smoldering cheroots. Clay had wrapped each cigar near its burning tip with a small piece of primer cord. He waited, checking the minute hand on his watch. Suddenly the primer cord sputtered into life on the first cigar, within seconds, on the second stogie.

"Good," muttered Clay. He scribbled on a small piece of paper.

He added more bits of primer cord and repeated the experiment several times. Satisfied, he returned to the livery.

The second horse offered by the stable owner—a big gray—looked good, but Clay wanted to test it and the saddle first. Unnoticed, he rode west out of town past the trail cutoff where he'd entered from the mountains that morning. He turned south into the desert before spurring the mare into a gallop. She moved faster and faster, revealing speed and endurance.

"You'll do just fine," he said, patting the horse.

Back in his hotel room, Clay closed his curtains, locked the door and wedged a chair under the knob. He opened his saddlebag and removed a canvas bag, dumping a disassembled sawed-off shotgun onto the bed. He oiled and cleaned the parts. Then, eyes closed, assembled and stripped the short-stock weapon several times.

Eyes open and using his sharp hunting knife, he bored a hole in the stock and looped a leather strap through the opening, twisting it securely around his right wrist. Opening the 12-gauge with his right hand and thumb . . . and using only his left hand . . . he loaded and unloaded the double-barreled shotgun several times, pulling shells from the big pockets of his new shirt. Satisfied, he broke the weapon apart, stuffed it in the canvas bag, and returned it to the saddlebag's right pouch.

From the other side of the saddlebag, Clay removed a coil of primer cord. He carefully unwrapped a bundle of candle-length red sticks, two small cans of black powder, and several small objects.

"It's all here," he said. He carefully tied the sticks into several small bundles, and returned them to the saddlebag.

Satisfied, he stretched out on the squeaky bed and slept.

It was late evening when Clay left the hotel and moved down the dimly-lighted street to the stable. The saddlebag sagged over his shoulder. Fort Henry's two saloons were busy. Their dirty windows splashed more shadows than light onto the board sidewalk. Sleepy horses lined the rails. An occasional wagon rattled past. Pianos played, and drunken men and women laughed and shouted. Other men stumbled from one noisy saloon to the other.

Two shadowy figures, with badges and rifles, quietly smoked and chatted outside the tower housing Durango's cell. A sliver of yellow light flickered through the barred window facing the street and town.

Clay wanted to talk with Durango, to reassure his old friend. But that was impossible.

He led his two horses out of the stable, shifted his rifle to the new mount—the big gray—and rode west, leading Mesquite.

It was near midnight when he returned, but without the big gray. He didn't return Mesquite to the livery stable. He quietly led the horse inside the Fort.

The Fort was cluttered with numerous buggies and wagons. A few men hovered over small fires swapping lies and bottles.

The same fat guard with a badge leaned on the wall near Durango's cell, his head lowered, occasionally moving, trying to stay awake. A lantern cast light near his feet.

Tying Mesquite in a far corner, Clay removed his boots, opened one side of his saddlebag, and quietly climbed one of the towers. He moved along the Fort's inside catwalks.

ft

A mixture of gray and orange light touched the dawn as Clay awoke to the smell of coffee and the sound of metal scraping metal. The iron bar and padlock on Durango's cell door was being removed. The heavy door clanged and squeaked defiantly as it was opened. Clay watched from under his blanket where he had spent a restless night on a pile of straw along the back wall of the Fort.

The fat guard with the badge wearily lifted his rifle and lantern. He joined another deputy carrying a pot of steaming coffee and a cloth-covered plate on a tray.

Durango must be eating better than when they were both jailed in Fort Henry, thought Clay. He, too, was hungry, and longed for some of the coffee.

The two men disappeared into the jail's stairwell, their descent silhouetted by the lantern's yellow circle of light.

Clay couldn't see Durango.

The men quickly emerged. They noisily slammed the heavy jail door and replaced the iron bar and lock. Canvas wagon flaps opened as curious sleepers within the Fort began to stir.

The two guards smiled, enjoying the attention.

Clay knew it wouldn't be long before all the vultures would be up, watching with hungry eyes, eager to see Durango die.

Clay's plan would need speed and precision, or he and Durango would be dead before the day began. He had planned and prepared. He only hoped it was enough. Now all he could do was wait for the precise moment. He swallowed the piece of jerky he'd been nervously chewing, then lighted a cigar, hampered by a light wind, and his shaking hand.

Clay's cigar was half gone before two other deputies drove a small flat-bed wagon onto the parade ground, circled their team and stopped under the beam spanning the Fort's entrance. A short man drove the field wagon, while his tall companion stood on the bed, and flung the noose over the high beam.

The tall deputy was McCarthy, Overstreet's handpicked hangman, the man who had tested the noose the day before. The squat driver was his same chinless sidekick.

The deadly loop swayed in the morning breeze.

McCarthy tossed the other end of the rope to the shorter man, who tied it to the side of the gate. McCarthy tugged on the noose. Satisfied, he climbed down.

Gray light spread across the Fort's parade ground as McCarthy and the two armed guards headed back toward Durango's cell.

The crouching sun was preparing to break from behind the eastern ridge of mountains.

Suddenly there was Durango, eyes blinking, adjusting to the morning light. He looked sullen, unshaven, and older than his young years. His hands were tied behind his back . . . his legs free. Two rifles poked into his back. He stumbled forward . . . toward the gawking crowd . . . men and women anxious to watch the execution.

Murder was a more fitting word to Clay.

Several men lifted small children onto their shoulders for a better look.

Clay caught Durango's frightened eyes for a fleeting second . . . and nodded. Then, again, pushed his hat back with his left index finger, repeating their recognition signal. Durango nodded and looked straight ahead. He walked stooped . . . his eyes red and glassy.

Durango knew Clay was there, that someone . . . a friend . . . might help. But . . . how? The morning light was brighter, an eager sun about to appear.

The crowd had grown larger as Durango was pushed forward, stumbling closer and closer toward the hangman's noose . . . and death!

The light wind increased, swirling dust around the wagon.

Durango was lifted onto the wagon bed, where he stood alongside a grinning McCarthy, who gripped the swaying noose.

The throng suddenly parted as a big man on a big horse approached the gate. A younger man wearing a black shirt and shiny badge rode alongside him.

The bigger man rode with a straight back and regal air. He wore a hat and tailored western suit—all white—complete with ruffled shirt, gold vest, black string tie and hand-tooled boots. A thick, hand-stitched gun belt circled his ample waist. The butt of a large pearl-handled pistol jutted from under his coat, gripped in its holster by a leather thong.

A white Bible filled the man's bear-claw left hand.

His round face was filled with pockmarks and power. His skin like aged beef. One side of his mouth drooped under a full mustache and inquisitive eye. A long tail of stringy gray hair dangled from the back of his head.

He stopped, but remained mounted next to the field wagon. His voice was quiet, but commanding.

"Deputy McCarthy," said the new arrival.

"Colonel Overstreet, sir," responded McCarthy.

The wind toyed with the cattleman's hat and hair. He gestured toward Durango.

"This the man killed Turk Donley?" asked Overstreet.

"Yes, sir," responded McCarthy.

Durango's tired eyes met those of the horseman.

Overstreet glared back, and pushed his horse through the crowd toward Durango. He thrust his Bible at the younger man, and growled: "Boy, the Old Testament says, 'An eye for an eye, a tooth for a tooth.' And the Ten Commandments say, 'Thou shalt not kill.'"

He leaned forward in the saddle and shook a thick finger in Durango's face. "But you murdered, boy!" he said. "You murdered!"

Durango shook his head. "No sir," he said. He straightened up, reaching his full six feet.

"Boy," said Overstreet, "if you've got any last words gnawin' at your hell-bound soul, spit 'em out, 'cause I'm out of time and patience." Durango stared up at the burly rider.

"I didn't murder anyone, Colonel," said Durango. His voice was firm. "Just defended myself against a drunk who had a knife. Same as you—or any man—would do. Killing Turk Donley was justified. Hanging me is murder. And you damn well know it."

Overstreet turned to his riding companion.

"Murder is murder, ain't it Sheriff?" he said.

"R-right. " stammered the sheriff.

"Well, then, do your duty, Sheriff," ordered Overstreet. "That's what you're paid for."

"Yes, sir." The sheriff fidgeted in the saddle, not sure what to do next.

"Well?" demanded Overstreet. "You can't hang Turk's killer if you're sittin' a horse!"

"N-no sir," stuttered the sheriff, red-faced.

The crowd chuckled.

It was time for Clay to act to save his friend—to set his plan in motion. He threw his dead cigar stub away, and, hand shaking, tried to light a fresh one. But his match broke against his trouser leg.

A second wooden match ignited but died before reaching his cigar. A cold wind snatched its flame, and kicked dust into the eyes of several bystanders.

Clay produced a third match.

Overstreet and the sheriff dismounted at the back of the wagon. The cattleman sneered in Durango's face.

The sheriff gave his orders. He and Durango were hauled up into the wagon bed.

Overstreet ignored McCarthy's helping hand and climbed up. The wagon sagged under his weight. He still clutched his Bible.

A guard gripped Durango's arm as the noose swayed above his head, responding to the wind. McCarthy braced himself behind Durango, his short, chinless partner, reins in hand on the wagon seat, steadied the wagon's pair of horses.

Overstreet and the Sheriff stood in front of Durango.

"Damn! This match better work," Clay murmured between set teeth. "Because if it doesn't . . ."

He didn't want to think about it.

The crowd was watching Durango.

Clay turned his back to the wind, cupped his hands and snapped the match tip with his fingernail. It ignited. He touched it to his cigar, and sucked in the smoke.

"Thank God," he sighed.

It was time.

Moving swiftly to the back of the fort, he slid behind a stack of discarded crates and barrels. He puffed hard on his cigar before wedging it between two logs, and wrapping a primer cord near the cigar's red tip. Clay lighted a second cigar and hurried to the wall behind the jail. He pressed the cigar into another crack, twisting primer cord around its smoldering tip.

Clay was ready.

He mounted Mesquite and reached into his saddlebag. He pulled out the canvas bag, stuffed his arm inside, and cocked the hammer on the sawed-off shotgun's right barrel.

The full morning sun suddenly crested the eastern mountain, shining its warmth, glory and blinding light across the fort's parade round into its wide gate.

The sheriff nodded. McCarthy dropped the noose over Durango's neck, and cinched it tight. He deliberately twisted the rough hemp, drawing blood.

Durango paled and choked. His legs twitched.

Overstreet grinned and leaned toward Durango. "Just a sample of what's comin', boy," he said.

McCarthy twisted the rope again, jerking the hangman's knot up behind Durango's left ear.

A black hood sagged in the sheriff's right hand . . . a hand that twitched nervously.

Overstreet held his Bible aloft with both hands and slowly turned to the crowd . . . and then to the heavens.

Everyone became silent. The only sound was the wind.

Overstreet closed his eyes, and spread his arms wide.

"Oh, Mighty God," he bellowed, his deep voice carried above the anxious throng. "Please accept the soul of this here man we're about to hang, because Lord, he's a blasphemous evil-doer—"

Overstreet's eyes snapped open, his words suddenly interrupted as an explosion on the fort's back wall scattered logs and debris. Then a trail of smoke raced up the side of the fort's north tower and wall, ending in two violent explosions, blowing the roof off the tower, ripping apart the catwalk and splitting the log wall.

The horses harnessed to the death wagon reared, pawing the air.

"Jesus!" cursed Overstreet, almost falling in the shaking wagon. He turned and stared open-mouthed toward the explosions.

Clay spurred Mesquite. The big horse galloped toward the wagon and open gate. Clay snapped his right wrist and let the wind suck the canvas bag from his sawed-off shotgun. Behind him, smoke sputtered up the jail-tower. It ended in an orange-and-black explosion that lifted the tower roof into the air, and blew another gaping hole in adjacent timbers.

A series of rapid firecracker explosions danced around the remaining front half of the fort's sagging catwalks. They ended in simultaneous explosions, disintegrating the catwalks and ripping off the tops of the last two towers at the front of the fort.

The short deputy desperately tried to hold the wagon's frightened team. Both horses reared and attempted to bolt.

"W-what the hell?" stammered Overstreet. He turned toward the morning sun—a blinding glare Clay hoped would protect him.

The crowd scattered as Clay neared the gate. Before charging under the cross beam he raised his shotgun and fired one barrel, disintegrating the rope above Durango's head.

"Durango, get down!" he yelled.

Durango threw himself forward onto the bed of the wagon, the noose further tightening around his neck, as the wagon team jerked free.

McCarthy and Overstreet were thrown on top of Durango. The deputy holding Durango toppled backward, landing on several surprised bystanders.

The sheriff lost his footing and tumbled over the edge of the wagon. He clutched the side panels. His boots dragged the ground as the wagon darted forward. Then half the side panel broke away, spinning the lawman into the dirt.

The driver pulled at the reins, but failed to control the panicked team.

As the wagon bolted through the gate, Clay raced alongside. His left hand grasped the bridle of the lead horse. He jerked the leather several times and, with strength he didn't know he had, guided the crazed team onto the road heading west from Fort Henry.

The chinless driver lashed out with his buggy whip, striking Clay in the chest.

Still gripping the bridle, Clay turned and, one-handed, deliberately fired the shotgun's second barrel into the empty half of the wagon seat. The driver slid sideways on the splintered wood and bounced. He yelled in pain, dropped the reins. clutched his bloodied hip . . . and tumbled backward off the speeding wagon.

Shouts and gunfire came from behind. A bullet sped past Clay's left ear. More gunfire. Another bullet bored a hole through the crown of his hat.

Overstreet struggled as he attempted to untangle himself from McCarthy and Durango. He waved his pearl-handled pistol at Clay as the bucking wagon tossed the trio like scrambled eggs. The cattleman steadied the pistol for a moment, then had it ripped from his hand when a wheel struck a rock, nearly flipping the careening wagon. The weapon bounced across the wagon bed several times, ending under Durango's legs.

Hogtied, face down, and unable to move, Durango gasped for air as the noose grew tighter and tighter around his neck. As Overstreet and the McCarthy struggled to right themselves against his body, the deputy's legs snared in the rope. With each attempt McCarthy made to free himself, the noose choked Durango more.

Clay heard Overstreet beseech God for mercy and divine intervention. Prayers that, for the moment, went unanswered.

With a flick of his right hand, Clay broke open the shotgun. His left hand plucked out the empty shells.

He freed the team. Letting the horses run on their own—riding alongside—guiding his own horse with his knees.

Clutching the shotgun, Clay tried to unbutton his shirt pocket with his free left hand to get more shells, but couldn't, prevented by his thick glove and the bouncing of his horse. He ripped off the glove with his teeth but still couldn't unbutton the pocket. He ripped it open, grabbed one shell, dropped the second, then caught it as it flipped in the air. He could get only one shell into the bouncing right-hand barrel. He closed the weapon with a snap of his wrist, and shoved his last shell into his pants pocket.

He reached out to grasp the bridle of the run-away team with his left hand, trying to control the careening wagon on the wash-board road, its human cargo clinging to the gyrating bed. The wide-eyed Overstreet, still loudly praying, clutched at the back of the wagon seat. The flat-bed jolted, swerved to the left, and—like a whip—snapped back as the road turned, dislodging McCarthy, who had untangled the rope from his legs. Saplings and brush abruptly terminated his flight. The bewildered hangman landed face down, shrouded in dust.

"Hold on Durango," yelled Clay. "We're almost at the cutoff."

They were out of rifle range . . . for the moment.

A bloodied McCarthy dragged himself out of the brush, limping and holding his left arm.

Clay glanced back. He could see a posse following.

Another five hundred feet and Clay would be at the creek and trailhead leading into the mountains. There his strength would be tested further. He twisted the strap from the shotgun tighter around his right wrist before turning the lathered team off the road. The old wagon clattered into the dry creek and shot up the far side. Its right rear wheel hit a boulder, shattering its wooden spokes and spinning the metal rim into the underbrush. Clay reined in his own horse and, using every muscle in his left arm, kept the wagon from climbing the bank.

Overstreet's meaty white hands gripped the back of the shattered wagon seat, his body rolled into a ball, knees under his chin. Sweat streamed over his tightly shuteyes and ran down his puffy, pale face.

"Sweet Jesus, sweet Jesus," prayed Overstreet between noisy gulps of air. He thanked God for deliverance.

Clay slid from Mesquite, climbed over Overstreet into the wagon, and cut the strap to his shotgun, freeing his right hand.

It took both Clay and Durango to loosen the choking noose from around Durango's neck. He coughed and sputtered. It took several deep breaths before Durango's red face regained some normal color. Clay shoved him off the shattered wagon onto his horse.

"Move! Move!" yelled Clay, slapping Mesquite's flank. Durango gripped the horse's neck as it struggled up the sandy riverbank onto the trail. The noose still circled Durango's rope-burned neck, the rope flailing behind.

The posse was closing. Its shots clipped the underbrush and ricocheted off the rocks.

Clay scrambled up the bank and cut the harness to the left horse of the wagon team. Gripping the horse collar, he struggled onto the animal's bare back.

"Hold it right there!" a deep voice yelled.

"What the . . ." started Clay, turning to his right.

Overstreet crouched behind the remains of the wagon seat, his pearl-handled pistol aimed at Clay's chest. Clay had almost forgotten the cattleman.

"Get your hands up" shouted Overstreet. He staggered off the shattered wagon, his white suit shredded and filthy.

Clay's sawed-off shotgun rested in his lap in his left hand, hidden from view.

Overstreet stood by the wagon.

"I should kill you!" he snarled. He thrust the gun at Clay, a horse-length away. "But seeing you hang , choking at the end of a rope will be better."

A deep cut crossed Overstreet's forehead. Blood flowed into his left eye.

"Hanging either of you damn drifters is fine with me," he said.

The blood clogged Overstreet's eye. Instinctively, he wiped at the blindness with his left hand.

Act now and possibly die, thought Clay, or die later.

Clay kicked his horse on his right against its teammate, its hooves throwing dust and gravel. As the animal spun on the creek bank, Clay ducked and, with his left hand in his lap, fired the shotgun's one loaded barrel at Overstreet.

The cattleman fired simultaneously, his aim distorted by dust and his bloodied eye. His shot went wild as the close blast from the 12-gauge shotgun ripped apart his gun hand and right shoulder. He yelled in pain as he was thrown backward into the dry riverbed.

"You won't be waving that hand in anybody's face, you sanctimonious bastard," yelled Clay. He spurred his horse up the bank.

Shouting, the posse left the main road and headed toward the creek. Deprived of one hanging they now had a chance to make it two. They wanted Durango back. They wanted Clay. And they wanted revenge!

Their shots hissed past Clay's head.

Overstreet struggled to his feet, clutching his mangled right hand. He stumbled toward the wagon, trying to avoid the onrushing posse. A rider's stirrup caught the cattleman's left side and spun him onto the safety of the crumpled wagon bed.

Clay yelled, leaned forward and forced the mare up the brushy trail, a zigzag of switchbacks and narrow ledges. At a sharp turn, he pulled his last shell from his pants pocket, almost dropped it, then shoved it into the shotgun's open breech. He fired downhill toward the riders crossing the creek, not expecting to do much harm, only hoping the blast and smoke might cover his escape.

The empty shotgun now a burden, Clay hurled it down at the posse. It spun like a rimless wheel, landing among the advancing horsemen, spilling one. Clay drew his pistol and fired into the pursuers.

Durango was near a cluster of boulders at the top of the trail.

"Wait at the rocks," yelled Clay. That's where he planned a big surprise for the posse.

Durango gave a quick wave. From there he could cover Clay's advance using the rifle from Mesquite's saddle-holster.

Deadly shots came closer as Clay's horse climbed the rocky trail. He gripped the animal's mane and harness, kicking it hard with his spurs. Riding bareback wasn't easy. The animal snorted and whinnied. Two hundred more feet and Clay would be safe.

Then shots came from above, puffs of white smoke from Durango's rifle. Deadly slugs whined above Clay's head toward the posse. One hundred more feet. Then fifty. The trail too steep for Clay to use his pistol—he needed both hands to stay mounted. Then the final exertion by the exhausted animal and Clay was over the top. He slid off the snorting beast and turned it, slapped its lathered rump, and sent it careening back down the trail.

Clay dropped behind the outcropping of boulders next to Durango.

The crazed horse plunged into the line of startled riders, their mounts tumbled and scattered in a melee of dust, rocks, legs and men. Durango and Clay added more shots to the confused scene.

Clay hurriedly brushed aside a thin layer of pine needles and dirt at the base of a trail-side boulder, uncovering a fuse leading to two red sticks of dynamite.

Durango made a clicking sound with his mouth.

"Clay, you're full of surprises," he said, rifle barking. The noose still dangled from his neck.

"Buried it riding in yesterday." Clay lit the short fuse. It sputtered and jumped toward the dynamite.

"Go! Go! Go!" yelled Clay, "Before she blows!"

The two fled along the flat mountain trail, Durango leading Clay's horse. At one hundred feet a loud explosion tore apart their abandoned boulder fortress. A landslide swallowed the slope and switchback trail, sending the posse scattering for their lives.

A cloud of brown dust and rocks filled the morning sky.

Farther along the trail, Clay stopped and caught his breath, then slipped behind two large pine trees. He retrieved a canteen and bag of food from a high limb.

"More surprises," said Durango.

Clay smiled. "A fresh horse is back there," he said, gesturing off the trail. "Tied him there last night."

Durango moved into the side canyon.

"Hey," yelled Clay. "You gonna keep that as a souvenir?"

Durango stopped and turned. "Keep what?" he said.

"That rope around your neck?"

"Well, I'll be damned." Durango's hand felt the noose and hangman's knot that swayed from his neck.

"You bet I'll keep it," he said, removing the noose. "Because without it, nobody—I mean nobody—is gonna believe what happened."

ft

Later, Clay was quietly enjoying a smoke, lost in thought as he rode Mesquite near the bottom of a rocky canyon. They were on the other side of the mountain, far from Fort Henry. He turned in the saddle.

"Durango," he said, "what in the hell were you doing in Fort Henry?"

"Went back for the jail food."

Clay shook his head.

"And to race my favorite cockroaches," added Durango.

"You're crazy," said Clay.

Durango smiled.

"Just passin' through," he said, "trying to stay out of trouble."

The mountain faded into the desert. Their horses trotted side by side.

Durango rubbed the deep rope burn on his neck, breaking their brief silence, again thanking Clay for saving his life. Then he looked puzzled.

"You know," said Durango, "I'd do the same for you."

"Do what?" questioned Clay.

"Save your life."

"I'd hope so."

Durango shook his head. "Only I'd do it faster," he said. He squinted into the afternoon sun.

"And Clay," he added, "don't you think you're getting a little long in the tooth for gun play and rescuing people? You're slowing down, too."

Clay's mouth fell open.

Durango nudged his horse ahead.

"And Clay," shouted Durango, "be more careful next time—somebody could get hurt!"

Durango laughed and spurred his horse into a gallop.

–The End–

Martin Hill Ortiz

Martin Hill? He is half-Latino. He currently resides in Puerto Rico. In Puerto Rico one's name formally honors both the father and mother; in this case, his father Milford Hill and his mother (maiden name) Adelina Ortiz. His name on official documents there is Martin Hill Ortiz and he often uses that as his pen name.

He is a professor of Pharmacology at the Ponce School of Medicine and Health Sciences in Ponce, Puerto Rico where he lives with his wife and son.

He has been writing seriously for over twenty years now. Awards and honors he has received include:

South Florida Writer's Association Poetry Award, 2nd place.
South Florida Writer's Association Poetry Award, 3rd place.
National Association of State Poetry Contests, 2nd place.
South Florida Writer's Association First Novel Award
Miami Representative to National Poetry Slam
Representative to the Los Angeles Poetry Festival
Science Fiction Writer's Association Poetry Contest, honorable mention.
Bewildering Stories, best story.
Frontier Tales, best story.

Martin has written four Suspense novels: *A Predatory Mind, A Predator's Game, Dead Man's Trail,* and *Never Kill A Friend*. He also produced *The Best Short Stories in the English Language*, Volumes I, II, and III. He's also had many examples of his short stories and poetry published online.

Find him at www. mdhillortiz.com

The Horse Whistle

by Martin Hill Ortiz

Pepper Mack sat on the root end of a toppled alamo near the brink of a ridge overlooking the town of San Rafael. The terrain below was painted with the blush of sunset. Pepper always enjoyed the sweet melancholy of the end of the day. Now was as fine a time as any to say goodbye to his old life.

Up until an hour ago, he sat alone. Then he was joined by the sheriff who straddled the trunk sitting an arm's length away. Together, they waited for Old Henry. If Old Henry appeared, Pepper would dance the noose jig.

"What kind of name is Pepper Mack?" the sheriff asked.

"Pepe McDonald, after my daddy."

"A confused parentage."

"Now, don't go attacking my folks. That's plain childish."

"Yeah, it is," the sheriff said. "Take this as my contrition." With a phfft, he launched a gob of chaw at Pepper's boots. "When did you start thieving horses?"

"I don't steal no horses." Pepper said, offended by the plural. He stole one only horse, over and over again.

Pepper and Old Henry had been zig-zagging west, hopscotching from town to town, aiming for Yuma in the Arizona territory. Pepper's daughter lived there along with his grandkids, three of them. Set up beside the mighty Colorado, Yuma had lots of rich mud for planting, a virtual paradise on earth. So he'd been told.

Old Henry was too old and bent to carry a load of cargo for much time—even one as scrawny as Pepper—so they walked side by side. Whenever their pilgrimage needed some funding—and that was often— Pepper sold Old Henry.

The night after the sale, Pepper would take to the road west of town. Upon finding a good lookout, he blew his horse whistle and waited. The whistle seemed silent but right off dogs took to howling. And, somewhere in the distance, Old Henry took note. The horse was clever, more clever than humans by half. Late at night, while his new owners slept, Old Henry would chew through his hemp or leather tie, then search out the weak spot on the fence or on the side of the barn.

Pepper would sometimes wait all night, in worst circumstances, two days. Eventually, Old Henry would chomp, squirm and bash his way to freedom, then plod off down the road to the sunset where the friends would reunite.

Together, they'd head off to the next town to pick up a few more dollars—a scheme that worked just fine until San Rafael.

ft

In the morning, when he and Old Henry ambled into town, they went straight to the master of the livery stables to announce a horse for sale. "He ain't got no gallop," Pepper said. "But he can still tow a plow." With the mention of "plow," Old Henry nickered and snarled.

Word went round about a cheap, shaky-kneed dray horse for sale. Several interested came by to look. Only two made offers, and those two fought.

"Thirty bucks," Dan Fowlkes said. "And he's not worth it." Old and mean, his face twisted so that his wrinkles criss-crossed. The crevices were filled with the grout of trail dust.

"Thirty-five, Mister," Nuff said. "I got it in Morgan silver." She jangled a purse. She was an ancient eighteen years of age, her clothes ragged and baggy.

"Don't go cross-bidding me," Dan said.

"I needs him more."

"Unless your brothers each plan on chomping on a shank of

horsemeat I suggest you need save your silver for food. I'll up you by five." Nuff pleaded to Pepper saying how she was caring for her four brothers, three to ten years of age. Since their parents died, she'd been selling off their ranch bit by bit to stay alive. They kept the valuable part, a productive well, but hauling water to their field took hours out of her day. She was sure Old Henry could change that and she didn't have the money for a more vital horse or mule.

Now, seeing that Pepper was choosing a victim, he much preferred the offer from Dan Fowlkes. It wasn't to be. Dan stamped his feet, cursed from high to low heaven but, after a lot of fist-waving, he withdrew his bids, all of his bids.

Pepper tried to tell Nuff that he wasn't ready to sell, but she wouldn't hear of it. For Pepper, he faced the inevitable arrival of the day when stealing might actually be wrong. Old Henry gave him an unforgiving stare.

ft

That evening as Pepper squatted on the alamo trunk, he was joined by Dan Fowlkes, the sheriff.

"I got sent a bulletin describing you and your game," he said. "I was waiting for you. Horse thieving is a capital offense hereabouts."

"Hereabouts and everywhere-abouts," Pepper said.

"I tried buying the horse myself but then I figured, what matter does it make? You try to chisel me or Nuff, I'll get back the dollars you stole and seize your nag, so nobody's the poorer. Except for you—but you'll be dead." He shot some brown spit into the earth.

"It ain't horse-thieving if I don't got no horse."

"It will be as soon as that old bag of bones arrives."

Pepper had not blown the whistle but Old Henry was a creature of habit and might just come anyway. The horse knew where to go—take the road out of town, into the sunset.

Out of obedience to that routine, Old Henry came strolling their direction. Pepper thought it would be a shame to die branded a thief. Even more of a pity to die innocent.

ft

When Nuff was ready to lead Old Henry away, Pepper looked his long-time friend in the eye and said, "Sorry, mi amigo. You's getting too old for the trail. Besides, them rich muds of Yuma they's my dream, not yours." He offered Nuff his whistle to be used in case Old Henry should stray.

"Lordy, lordy, look who's coming for a visit," the sheriff said. Although still a good fifty yards off, the silhouette and the slow lonesome shuffling of Old Henry were unmistakable.

Pepper thought about dying. At least Old Henry would live on with a nice family who needed him.

A long stone's throw away, Old Henry stopped and cocked his head. Dogs began barking. The horse turned and began loping home.

–The End–

D. L. Chance

The son of a Pentecostal minister, Donald L. Chance was born on ancestral homelands in South Carolina and grew up playing music in small churches all over the United States. He went on to a long and satisfying career as a professional musician (specializing in various styles of country and southern rock music) before giving in to another lifelong passion: the written word. Honing his writing skills with fiction was only natural, and led to combining his musical expertise with the journalism of his college days when he was asked to cover country music for his local paper.

Dozens of short stories and novels later, along with several thousand news and feature stories for several newspapers, wire services and magazines, Chance is enjoying following in the footsteps of his literary heroes such as Steinbeck, Twain and McMurtry. Currently, Chance is happily juggling careers in both music and writing, and not only has a new album of original songs (on which he played all the instruments himself) available for worldwide download, but a new collection of short stories ready for a summer 2018 release. He and his wife of 36 years live in North Texas.

A Shootout in Jerome

by D. L. Chance

A bullet, probably from an old Henry by the distinctive low-pitched echoes off nearby hillsides, cracked past Breck's ear to gouge a splintery groove along the barbershop's sun-silvered wooden wall.

Catching a glimpse of Jack Calloway at the corner of a hardcase saloon across the street, he stepped back into the doorway of the barbershop and propped his head back against the bare, unpainted jamb. Sweat trickled into his eyes and a thin trail of blood seeped down his left hand to drip onto the toe of his boot.

He felt it as each precious drop of his life raised a small dust cloud on the expensive custom-made boot he'd hastily slipped into before running into the sun-blasted street of Jerome, Arizona, and headlong into the bullet Calloway's now-dead brother Josh had managed to graze the fleshy part of his left forearm with before catching one of Breck's better-thrown rounds in the teeth. Josh lay in the dust just off the walkway, his boot heel still resting on the outer lip of the rough plank walk outside the barber's front door. Ignoring the occasional twitch of the recently departed outlaw's foot, Breck tried to make himself as skinny a target as any paint on the doorway would have been had the damn barber chose to paint it.

Again, he wished mightily for a smoke.

Pale, frightened faces peered out of windows all along the side of the street he could see from where he stood, but he knew there'd be little to no immediate help from the local citizenry in this dust-up.

Dammit! Why hadn't he thought to bring his damn double-hung gun belt rig to Arizona in the first damn place!

He silently calculated how many guns the Calloway Gang might have put into the field this hot mid-morning and wondered if he had enough rounds left in his Remington .44 to serve the entire bunch, as his extra shells were still sitting comfortably in his single-hung gun belt on the valise back in the tub room of this same barbershop. Probably not, he decided as a whiskey-rough voice shouted out from across the street.

"You got my brother, Hartfield," Jack Calloway screamed, enraged. "You just shot him down dead in the street, and I'm gonna kill you for that there and nothing else!"

"I'm much obliged," Breck called back, rattling the barber's door to make sure it was still locked behind him. "And I must say I'm right relieved by the generosity. I'll just take it you're going to forgive me for busting up your rustling business then?"

An infuriated gurgle came from the area of the saloon corner across the way.

"I'm gonna kill you slow for ever drawing breath on this world, Hartfield!"

"I don't wonder, I reckon." Breck noted a shadow movement in the heavily painted front window of a cafe next to the saloon. He nodded to himself. "And here I thought you had some Christian charity in you, Jack Calloway," he yelled, "but I guess I was wrong. A Hartfield don't like being wrong, Jack." He'd need to expose at least an arm to get a clean shot at the cafe, and a long pistol shot it looked to be, too. But it beat making such a dandy target himself by stepping all the way out from his scant cover.

On the other hand, though . . .

"Say, I lost count," he suddenly shouted. "How many things is that you're gonna kill me for, again?"

The shadow crept slowly toward the middle of the window, the shape of a rifle barrel obvious in the backlit silhouette. Breck guessed the gunhand must be figuring to smash out the glass then jump through, levering rounds as he came.

A stupid plan.

"See," Breck continued almost conversationally in his raised voice,

"I'll lay down in peace knowing just how many scores you managed to settle with me today. Hey, do you boys mind if we call a little truce so I can take a minute and hunt up a smoke?"

Calloway set up an incoherent bout of furious cursing, then pegged a shot at the doorway. His bullet smashed the front bracket holding the "Barber" sign over the door. The signboard suddenly swung loose, missing Breck's face by the thickness of a good coat of shaving lather, and swayed halfway free on its remaining eyebolt. The hidden rifleman threw another useless round at the wooden false front, nicking the sign on its outward trip and spinning it a half-turn. The bastard had a lousy eye for shooting, Breck decided.

"Dammit, Hartfield," Calloway bellowed, "I'm gonna—"

Breck stepped onto the boardwalk and threw a quick shot at the cafe window, starring the painted glass at the place where the lurking shadow's chest clearly stood. Then, ignoring the commotion his single bullet touched off inside the eatery, he calmly turned toward where Jack Calloway was all but dancing in the dirt alongside the saloon's wide porch overhang. Slowed by his wounded arm, Breck knew he'd missed the outlaw boss as soon as the Remington bucked in his fist.

The rustler/killer had time to widen his eyes and fall to the dust, then slither back into the narrow dark space between the saloon and the brick building next door before Breck's tardy slug chewed a splinter from the wooden corner of the saloon just over his head.

"Damn," Breck muttered. One less round, should things get truly interesting directly.

Calloway returned the lead, drilling a hole through the hanging sign and setting it to swinging again.

"Dammit," he railed, "you ain't decent people, Hartfield!"

"I reckon not."

The most interesting thing to Breck about the one-sided gunfight was the fact he hadn't cared at breakfast this very morning one way or another just what the Calloway brothers and their sundry collection of bar loafers and murderous saddle tramps might be up to in the mountains and valleys near Cleopatra Hill. The Hartfield's family business, out of Denver, dealt only with those who could boast the deep pockets necessary to buy the specialized set of extremely sensitive and dangerous services the family provided. Rustlers, claim jumpers, and even Jack Calloway's brand of mean but smalltime murderers were strictly petty operators—matters for local law enforcement.

But the town marshal had apparently decided to go fishing up in the hills with the local sheriff when it was learned that one of the famous Hartfield brothers had turned up in Jerome and looked none too happy. They didn't even stop to find out which brother, or why he wasn't the perfect picture of good cheer.

"You know, Jack," Breck called out, "most men'll nerve themselves up to try shooting a Hartfield just because they think it'll get their name in one of those silly yellowback books." He wiped sweat from his eyes, as his Stetson was keeping company with his spare ammunition inside and the sun on his uncovered head was a hot, heavy hand. "But I don't reckon you can even read, can you?"

Calloway answered with more lead.

"Didn't think so."

A new shot, an even wider miss from the unseen rifleman with the Henry, placed the would-be sniper in a different spot now. Moving around for a better angle, Breck knew he'd need to keep a better ear out for that one.

John Breckinridge Hartfield had come to Arizona Territory a week back for the sad funeral of an old friend. On his way home, tired and dusty after a long night of bouncing over the Mingus Mountain stage road from Prescott, he decided to lay over at the breakfast stop in Jerome and get a shave and bath, and maybe a nap, before starting the rough trip downhill to Cottonwood, where he could catch the Flagstaff train up from Phoenix. He would have left Jerome on the noon stage if the brash and reckless Josh Calloway hadn't recognized him and braced him inside the very barbershop at his back.

"You ain't a very forgiving man, are you, Jack?"

"Damn you, Hartfield!"

"You already did."

Though he'd never laid eyes on them in his life, Breck had heard of the Calloway brothers, and recognized them almost on sight. A successful man in his business made it a point to learn just who might, and who might not, be interested in filing his notch to a sidearm—and besides his brother, Cole, or Coldheart to those who had reason to fear him, there were lonesome few other successful men in his line of work.

According to the wanted posters the family kept on file at the Hartfield offices, Jack, the elder Calloway, habitually wore his graying beard thick and unkempt to hide a badly broken and poorly healed jaw. But the crooked jaw line was still unmistakable. Pale, colorless eyes peering out of all the hair made Jack look every bit as mean as he in fact was, even if he wasn't all that great a shot.

The late Josh Calloway was different. With no unusual facial features saving dull, blank eyes and a weak chin, Josh was wiry and fast and accurate with his irons. But the chinless baby brother couldn't claim ownership to even half of what Jack used for intelligence. Breck was still amazed the skinny sumbitch even recognized him in the barber chair.

Jack and Josh had been run out of Colorado a few years back for plying their lethal trade among the mining districts west of Trinidad. Even so, Breck never bore them any personal hard feelings. Until now.

The rifle spoke again, the shot breaking out one of the small panes of glass in the barber's front window. Breck heard a sudden intake of breath from behind the solid plank door at his back and smiled, his fair-featured face turning into something cold and dangerous. The soft jangle of a spur inside the shop widened the grin into a frosty grimace of deadly determination.

And he casually noted the smoke belched out by the Henry was still hanging in the calm heat behind a water trough just to the right of the cafe.

Carefully, Breck slipped the three empty shells from the Remington's well-oiled cylinder and palmed them. Then he thumbed back the hammer to full cock.

Time to put an end to this foolishness.

"Jack," he called out, "if I don't make it, here's a few souvenirs for you two boys that're left, but I don't want you smoking my cigars." He tossed the spent hulls onto the boardwalk. "You can tell folks they're from J. Breckinridge Hartfield's last dance."

On the rough wood planks of the walk, near Josh's worn-out boot heel, the brass cartridges lay glittering in the relentless sun. Calloway and his rifleman had no way of counting how many there had been.

"Breckenridge? Hell, Josh swore you was Coldheart when he saw you step off that stage," Calloway shouted. "Ignorant bastard. But I reckon any Hartfield will do me. Watch him, Dude," he called out to his sniper, "he's reloaded now, and I heard this'n's just as handy with the iron as his big brother. Kinda like me'n Josh—damn!"

Breck stepped from the deep doorway and turned to drill a slug through the door behind him. A quick return bullet punched splinters off the thick planks of the boardwalk less than a foot from Breck's left boot and went whistling off across the street. Inside, a body fell heavily, heels drumming on the floorboards and spurs jingling merrily.

Before the needle-tipped wood shards even fell back to hit the barber's dusty threshold, Breck stepped smoothly out onto the walk to pump a round at the rifleman before swinging his Remington toward Jack's position.

The sniper screamed and threw a battered old Henry rifle over the trough and out into the dirt. "You got me, Hartfield," he cried, his hands springing into the air. "I'm coming out."

"Good," Breck yelled, his eyes never leaving the area where Jack Calloway still lay under cover. "Stand polite by that cafe door yonder, and you might live to get to prison."

"I will!" Holding his left hand to a uselessly dangling right arm, a weasel-faced little creature in spectacles and a dusty derby lurched to his feet and staggered over to stand near the painted cafe window. "Yes sir!"

"I said stand by the door!"

"Yessir!" The outlaw slithered over to stand quaking next to the café entrance. "I'm here."

"Now stay there." Breck then ignored the man. His eyes narrowed as he thumbed back the hammer again—an unusually loud noise in the silent, empty street. "Jack," he called, "you're the last one. I can see you from here. Are you gonna join this here pardner of yours in Yuma, or your brother in the graveyard?"

"Damn you," Calloway shrieked. "How the hell'd you know there was just the five of us, Hartfield?"

Breck let out the deep breath he'd been holding, silently thankful his hunch—the strange talent that had seen him more or less safely through so many of these silly tragedies—had served him yet again.

"Because I'm a Hartfield, Jack Calloway," he yelled back, unusually proud of the fact for some fool reason. "A Hartfield."

Calloway lay quietly in the shaded dust for what felt to Breck, standing in the direct heat of the sun without his hat, like a long, long time. Then the badman cussed.

"I heard you damned Hartfields never shoot a man when he's showed he's through. That the fact?"

"That's the fact."

Another longish time crawled by. Then a battered old Peacemaker flew out to kick up dust in the street. Again, Breck heaved a sigh of relief.

Keeping the muzzle pointed directly on the spot where Calloway would appear, Breck walked out and picked up the tired, oft-repaired Henry and checked its load. He nodded, satisfied. Retrieving the heavy old Peacemaker, with its six live ones in the wheel, he let the fat but deadly rounds fall to the dirt at his feet. Then he tossed the now harmless old weapon over his shoulder. He cocked the Henry and moved it to his stiffening left hand.

"You ready now, Jack?"

"I reckon I am, dammit!"

"You gonna give me trouble?"

"Hell, you got all the guns."

"Then let's go."

Jack Calloway came slowly to his feet. Breck motioned for the former would-be sniper, Dude, to walk forward and stand in the street in front of the saloon. More faces were appearing at windows up and down the street, and a few brave souls were even venturing out onto the walkways.

As if in a nightmare he couldn't quite wake from, Jack walked forward to stand next to his last living partner.

"I got your word, Hartfield," he said, his eyes narrowing suspiciously when Breck didn't lower the Remington. "You gave me your word you wouldn't shoot."

"Yeah." Breck suddenly lifted his .44 and pointed it at a spot between and above Jack Calloway's wild eyes. At this, Dude began blubbering and fell to his knees in the dust. "I did, didn't I?"

"N-Now, Hartfield," Jack stuttered, "even you wouldn't shoot me down in front of all these here witnesses." His voice became almost a wail. "You wouldn't do that!"

"Let's have the other gun, Jack."

"Other—" Breck thumbed back the Remington's hammer. "Oh! I plumb forgot that one!" Calloway reached gingerly inside his loose-fitting shirt and brought out what looked like a grimy Starr five-rounder. He tossed it across to Breck. "Here you go," he said amiably. "You can point that cannon somewheres else now."

But the unsmiling eye of Breck's Remington never wavered.

"They found a rancher by the name of Pete Martin on his range over in the Chino Valley a couple weeks back," he said softly. "Pete had better than a dozen bullet holes in him." A look of animal rage came over Breck's otherwise affable-featured face. "By the damage to the corpse, some of those holes came from a Henry. Then it looked like someone stood up real close and shot him in the back after he was already down and dying. He was found still looking over his shoulder at whoever done it. I don't suppose you gents'd know about any of that, would you?"

The sniper's hands suddenly flew to his face. He fell over on his side, sobbing like a child.

Jack Calloway swallowed back a huge gulp. "I . . . we don't get over into the Chino Valley much. Didn't. Didn't get over into the valley."

"You got 'em, mister," someone shouted from the walk in front of the saloon. "Put that smoker down now."

A woman in the gathering crowd agreed. "Killing unarmed men is just plain old murder," she called out.

Breck ignored the bystanders. Instead, his finger whitened as he put pressure on the trigger mechanism—a lethal movement Jack could hardly miss. "Pete Martin was my friend," he said softly. "Now I'm gonna ask you again. Do you know anything—"

"Hellfire, we did it, Hartfield!" Muscles in Calloway's crooked jaw worked furiously, rippling his nasty beard as he glanced around at the growing crowd. "We did it. Hell, that's our job. Rustling. That Martin bastard just came along when he should'a stayed at the house." Calloway half-turned and threw a vicious kick at his openly weeping gunhand. "Damn your worthless ass, Dude. I told you over and over to get rid of that damn museum antique you shoot!"

"B-But it was my Granddaddy's," Dude bawled, half-heartedly returning the kick. "In the war, he—"

"Hey," Breck bellowed, tapping lightly on the side of Calloway's head with the Henry's long barrel, "there's plenty of time for that when y'all get together with Josh there in hell directly."

Calloway looked back at Breck, and the steady muzzle of the unforgiving weapon, and gulped again. "I told you what you want, Hartfield," he bellowed. "I confessed! We done it, and I'm not denying it. Now park that damned cannon, dammit!"

Breck's eyes narrowed.

"Dammit, Hartfield, you gave me your damn word! Put it down. I told you what you wanted, and in front of these here witnesses, too. Put the damned cannon up now! I told you—"

Breck pulled the pistol's trigger.

The hammer clicked loudly on an empty chamber.

Calloway reacted to the dry snap as he would have if Breck had actually shot him—he screamed and fell backwards over his partner.

Onlookers gasped like the faithful watching a miracle in church.

"I reckon you did tell me at that, Jack Calloway," Breck said, sighing. Casually, he passed the revolver to his left underarm and pointed the Henry in the direction of the heaped-up outlaws. "And these people can all testify in court to your confession. But at least now you know how Pete Martin felt watching someone drop the hammer on him." Turning to the townspeople, he raised his voice. "If someone wants to go round up your town law now, I'd sure appreciate it."

A couple of men took off running up the hilly street toward the partially treed upper end of town.

When he could talk, Calloway gazed into Breck's now calm face. "But I saw you reload that piece, Hartfield. How come—"

"You saw me get rid of empty shells," Breck said, shaking his left arm to keep down the stiffness. "I didn't have anything to reload with. They're all with my clothes back in the barber's tub room."

Calloway wouldn't let it go. "Then where's that sixth round?" he wailed. "Where's the damned sixth round?"

A grin spreading on his face, Breck winked at the outlaw boss. "Now you know it ain't safe to carry but five rounds in a sidearm you ain't about to put to immediate use," he said lightly. "Hell, anyone knows that."

Breck watched as Calloway mentally counted off his shots.

One bullet served Josh. Number two went into the gunny hiding inside the café—they were just hauling his corpse out into the street now—and number three chipped wood off the saloon corner above Jack's head. The backshooting bastard inside the barbershop—barbers don't usually wear spurs when they're working, and don't generally have call to shoot a paying customer in the back anyway—must've caught round number four somewhere around the breastbone, and number five clipped that piece of meat off the bespectacled rifleman's right shoulder. Jack Calloway's eyes became the size of buffalo pies.

"Then, when you made me surrender just now, you was . . ."

Breck shrugged. "Armed only with my good looks and righteous intentions, Jack." Then his smile slipped. "But still, Pete Martin was my friend."

Calloway's eyes narrowed dangerously. "Now how in hell could you have knowed we did that one?"

Breck merely stared at him.

"Dammit! How did you know, Hartfield?"

They were just fetching out the body from inside the barbershop, and Breck felt a welcome relief seeing he'd been right about this one too. The backshooter turned out to be a big ugly bastard with a hard-used double-hung holster rig, slung low and ready for deadly chores he'd never again have reason to do.

Armed men came up and jerked the live outlaws to their feet, but Jack Calloway kept his wild eyes on Breck.

"Hartfield! How did you know?"

"You told me, Jack," Breck said, noting the belated arrival of the town law. "Just now. See, I was only guessing 'til then."

Despite two men holding onto him, Calloway slumped to his knees in the dusty street, muttering curses at everything and everyone in sight.

Breck eased the hammer down on the Henry, then passed it to an old man wearing a town marshal's badge. He shoved his Remington into his belt. Needing a Carolina desperately, he turned his back on the outlaws and walked toward the barbershop to get the bath he'd come there for in the first place. Behind him, Jack Calloway screamed again.

"Hartfield!"

–The End–

Willy Whiskers

Calliope Gazette, June 18, 1910. For as long as anyone here remembers, a bearded gentleman has prowled the streets of Calliope befriending souls, tending to the community's business, and extolling the exploits of our residents. Of course, we refer to Willy Whiskers; William Grafton Bonifantie. We suspect none of our readers knew Willy by that name. He came to Calliope in 1870 as the engineer of Engine 75 from the old Nevada Central Railroad (NCRR), later he became our beloved constable.

"Couldn't have done my job without him," said retired sheriff Billy Blowbag.

"We love him here," said Savanna Sal at the Peachtree when we interviewed her and her friend, Betsy Loving. "When Willy gets to telling his tales there's always a lively crowd around his table. Most folks are scared of being included in his stories, but they get mighty bent if they aren't."

Our school principal, Mrs. Dorothy McCallian, said, "Willy is like a Homer for all the people. There is no better sight then the light in my students' eyes when he comes to class and talks to them of the old days in Calliope."

When we asked Willy where his stories originated, the normally loquacious yarn-spinner said "Oh, I just tell them like they wish it was." Still making his rounds, we look forward to hearing from Willy for many years to come.

Calliope Gazette, December 8, 1923: At 69 years and in failing health, Willy Whiskers told his last tale.

The Witch and the Gandy Dancer

by Willy Whiskers, Constable of Calliope, NV

Long before Calliope was a town or even a village it was a mining camp—
or at least there was a mining camp up in the hills overlooking the town
as it stands today. As silver strikes go, the Calliope lode did not rival
the Comstock, but it did attract its share of starry-eyed diggers. Among
them were Jacob Miller and his wife Andorra. Jake worked the mine
and his wife took in laundry and ran a lunch table jammed between two
ramshackle saloons.

Andorra was taller than most women, broad shouldered, but not
handsome. The life of a miner's wife was far from comfortable so it was
necessary to develop a hard skin, though she probably had one already,
otherwise she would not have been among the scarce number of women
in the territory. As such, she gained the reputation as an unpleasant
person. No one went to her for feminine comfort and it was only for need
of a meal that any miner came near her at all.

An errant blast deep in the mine sent Jake to his treasure in the sky.
When they told the now-Widow Miller, she stood still for a moment,
stared off into the abyss, and went right back to dishing out stew to a table
full of miners. It was couple of years before the mother lode played out
and the big mining interests moved in. They were the only ones who could
make a go of the lower grade ore. By then, Andorra was living in a one-
room hovel above the old mine and for all evidence had no income at all.

Among the residents of the nascent town, the Widow Miller was a
curiosity. Every few weeks one general store or another would send a

clerk up the hollow with the meagerest of supplies. No one ever saw the woman—she would leave a few coins in a tin can tacked to the cabin door and speak to the errand boy through a closed window. Occasionally a trespasser came too close to her domain and his first warning was a shotgun blast or a rifle shot too close to be misunderstood.

Everyone in town had at least one Widow Miller story. The two most prevalent were that she was from Salem and therefore a witch. It was true she was from Salem—Salem, Indiana—and that she had a horde of gold and silver hidden in the floor of her cabin. She was said to incessantly count it from dark to dawn. Without any real knowledge about her, the tales ran wild.

One night Tommy Worth, Eli Roule, and a few other boys got into some of Tommy's father's hard cider and decided to see how close they could come to the old woman's shack before getting a warning blast. Eli mentioned, "If we're lucky we might catch her counting then we can snatch some of her gold." Moving quietly, or as quietly as a bunch of half-drunk young men could, they picked their way up the steep dark path to their destination. In the distance they saw a faint light from a single lamp peeking thought the shuttered window. This encouraged them.

They reached the building undetected. They knew they were undetected as they had not been shot. Once there, they had no idea what to do next. Tommy would later tell how he stood up and yelled at the house, "We've come for your gold!" then they all rushed the door only to find it barred from inside. He went on to say they heard the widow witch chanting some incantation and the whole cabin erupted into blinding light. Confident in their successful sortie they all high-tailed it back to town, falling and skidding their way down the hill. Tommy was the only one who ever talked openly about that night and for some reason the members of small gang were never close after that.

By the time they reached home, the whole town was aware of a fire at the top of the hollow. The blaze filled the sky and several men mounted up to investigate. Reaching the widow's shack they found it totally engulfed and in no time just a pile of smoldering ashes. In the morning, they found the remains of a person they assumed was Andorra, wrapped her in a canvas and brought her down to the new cemetery east of town. All that remained was burned kitchen gear, two tins of coins dated to the time of the silver strike, and what was left of her bed—nothing else.

The passing of the Widow Miller might have ended the stories, but being such a horrendous local event, it just fueled more outlandish yarns. If she was a witch, then her death would not stop her—she would be out for revenge against Tommy and the boys or the people of the town or even the town itself. Her grave became taboo and the next generation of youth looking to prove themselves would visit it with cider—or whiskey—filled bellies. By the time the gandy dancer Abel Hammond came to town to work on the railroad there was a very rich and intricate folklore surrounding the Widow Miller.

Abel was a smallish man, wiry, with a shock of light tan hair and narrow squinty eyes. You could pick him out amidst the section gang as if he was a child among men. If this was not peculiar enough, Abel was afraid of just about everything: snakes, bugs, the number 13, spilling salt, everything. But the one thing that scared him most was graveyards. He would walk three streets out of his way just to miss a tombstone.

Most cowboys had their favorite saloon. In the days of the cattle drives in Kansas, the drovers would park their chuck wagons out in front of their chosen bar to mark their headquarters. The same can be said of the railroad men. In a town with one saloon for every ten people barmen were grateful for the loyal business of a section gang or two.

The boys at the Full Mug saloon were railroad men and a nastier bunch than most. Unfortunately for Abel, he was on their crew and they showed him no mercy. They had endless fun setting him up, doing things to make him panic, piss his pants, or just bolt and run all the way home. Why he continued to visit that pub is a mystery, but I think if you asked him he would say they were his friends.

In many western towns, the cemetery had an exotic name, like the famous Boot Hill. In Calliope, we just called it the graveyard and one fateful night the Full Mug boys fixed on the subject of graveyards and pestered Abel about what bothered him about the place. Of course, Abel's fears had no reason and he just said, "I didn't like them."

"Well, it's just time to face your fears and we'll help you," said Jacko, the gang foreman. The typical big Irish bully, he was unkempt, shaggy and sported a pair of the largest hands granted any man.

"Oh, no." Abel looked down with his hunched shoulders. "You couldn't pay me to go there."

"Oh, yes. And we will do just that very thing. Come on men. Let's get up a poke for Abel." Jacko passed his hat all round and it soon jingled with coins. The barman promised a week of free drinks. "Here it is, it's all for you. All you have to do is go into the graveyard and come out."

Abel was amazed. This was the most positive attention they had ever granted him. He started feeling like he was one of them. "Just step in the graveyard?"

"Pretty much, " granted Jacko. Then Harry, the one they called Professor because he had finished 8th grade, spoke up. "No, you will have to go to the back of the yard. This is a pretty heavy purse. If you want it you need to earn it."

"The Widow Miller's grave is back there," added Peter. He was a weasely, twitchy man who always jumped into these schemes once a few others had already preceded him. "You have to go that far."

Abel's new found courage began flagging. "The Widow Miller? She was a witch. I'm not going anywhere near her."

The local lore was strong and Abel believed every word. The stories of her death and about her ghost out for revenge spoke directly to the fearful man. No amount of whistling past the graveyard was going to make him feel any better about this proposal.

"Come, come, Abel. You can't live in fear all your life. This could be a watershed for you. Your whole life could change. Don't you want that?" Jacko put his arm around the small man and gave him a playful punch in the jaw.

In the end, Abel agreed and would visit the grave that very night. As he left the tavern Harry stopped him. "Just a minute. We have to have some proof that you went."

Handing Abel a broken chair leg, he said. "When you get to the grave, just hammer this stake in the ground so we will know you were there." Abel took the stake and headed out. Moving into the darkness he heard laughter coming from the bar.

Screwing up his courage, Abel pulled his long coat around him as a comfort and headed straight for the graveyard. The moon was half full so there was some light, but not much. The sky was full of fast-moving puffy clouds that caused shifting shadows to play across every surface. Reaching the graveyard he hesitated, but he wanted to make good on his task for some reason. Perhaps he wanted to show his manhood, or he really wanted to conquer his fear, or the money drove him. Whichever, he made his first few halting steps. Happily there were no adverse effects, so he pushed on.

It was not long before he arrived at the small wooden marker with the widow's name roughly scribed on it. This was not her original grave marker. That had been stolen, and the next one desecrated, then one was burned, and another just disappeared. The present rough board was the handy work of Eli, who used to work in the mines until his health gave out and now lived in an old cabin in the hollow, not far from the spot of the widow's place.

Abel looked around in the faint light and for the first time in his life he felt calm at a time when he would be nearly paralyzed with fear. Facing his terrors had filled his chest with power and confidence. His backbone stiffened. His lungs filled full for the first time. He stood tall.

"Just one more thing to do," he thought in his new found swagger. Dropping to his knees he pulled out the stake and placed the tip on the ground. Pushing hard to drive it into the earth, he found it did not penetrate. A few more efforts brought no additional effect. Feeling around, he found a small cobble. Using it as a mallet, he brought the stone down several times on the stake driving it into the dirt. One last hit made it good and secure—it was time to leave. He mind was full of collecting his prize and finally facing down his tormentors.

Moving to rise, something held him down. Abel tried again to gain his feet with no success. Once more, and again and again he tried, but whatever had him held him fast. Forgetting about all his new-found courage, only visions of the old witch filled his mind.

"Let me go!", he screamed, "Let me go!" He continued pulling and pulling, but he was still stuck fast. "I didn't kill you. You don't know me. Let me go!" Suddenly he felt a hand grabbing his arm and another on his leg. He knew the witch was pulling him into the grave. This sent him into a new panic, more terror than he had ever felt before. "Let me go, Let me go, let me go . . ."

Back at the tavern everyone forgot about Abel and the evening passed away. It was several days before anyone wondered why Abel wasn't around. He had often missed work in the past, so no one thought much of it at first.

"I wonder if he went to the grave," said Jacko as the first round of drinks hit the table.

"Let's go see," added Peter.

The railroad men all rose in unison, grabbed their mugs, and in solemn procession trudged up to the graveyard. It was placed on a hill and no one could see the widow's grave from the road as it was on the back side, so they all had to make their way inside. None of them would admit it, but their hearts beat faster and each felt uncomfortable among the graves.

At the witch's grave they found Abel's cold body laid out on its back. He was a sad sight starting to show the decay of a man three days dead. Jacko and the boys felt a little ashamed at having a hand in sending the little man to this place. Say what you will, Abel was still one of them, as the runt of the litter is still a member of the pack.

Solemnly, they wrapped his long coat around him and buttoned it tight. Each grabbing a handful of cloth, they lifted him. Or at least they tried, for there was something holding him to the ground. That is when the Professor found the broken chair leg piercing the coat through one corner as proof of Abel's triumph over his fears.

–The End–

Nancy Peacock

Several years ago, I began writing novels which solved the problem of what to do with the stories swirling around inside my head. I couldn't type fast enough. It was strange to watch the characters take on a life of their own. Occasionally they would dictate where the story was going. I write what I like to read—no fillers, no excess verbiage, no great philosophical depths. I like my characters, even the ones I kill off. There is a little bit of my own experiences in every story. I've been reading since I was four. I'm never bored with a book in my hand.

Unfinished Business

by Nancy Peacock

Editor's Choice

Jack reined his horse at the edge of the clearing. He had veered off the trail to ride through the woods when a faint whiff of wood smoke had alerted him to the presence of people. He was too tired to get careless now. No sense riding directly into a mess if he could help it. He stretched a little taller in the stirrups to see over the scrub cedar that concealed him. Below was a cabin surrounded by oak trees, a barn, corral, kitchen garden and a field with the stubble of a corn crop. A good three acres were plowed, ready for a spring crop. His first thought was that someone had put in many hours of work to create such a place. Rock walls spoke of hard labor clearing the fields. A few boulders jutted out in awkward places. He remembered his father saying that some rocks might be the tips of mountains and should be left alone. He had plowed around a few of those in his youth.

A movement in front of the house caught his eye. A figure was leading a bay horse along, but a tree blocked his view for a moment. When the figure emerged into the open, he saw that the horse was dragging something he couldn't identify. He exited the cover of the woods and let his horse amble toward the cabin. His rifle was loose in the scabbard; his revolver was in his hand. As he neared the barn, he saw three horses with saddles on them in the corral. He pulled up short and stared. These were the horses he had followed across miles of rugged terrain to arrest their owners for murder and arson. Why would any rider let his horse loose in a corral and leave the saddle on? Why not just tie it to the rail in front of the cabin? Were the men he wanted inside?

The only way to find out was to press on. Something was definitely wrong. He spurred his horse closer to the cabin which caught the attention of the small woman leading the bay. She held a rifle awkwardly in one hand and the reins of the bay in the other. She looped the reins around her arm to free her hands, raised the rifle and held a steady bead on him.

He called, "Ma'am, I mean you no harm." He slipped the revolver into his pocket and held his hands high to show he had no firearm aimed at her. She never wavered. He took his eyes off her for a second and recoiled at the sight of what she was dragging. A man, face down, tied by the feet to a long rope. His shirt was bloody on the back.

Jack stepped down from his horse and stared. Without considering what the consequences might be, he said, "What on earth are you doing?"

The woman kept the rifle aimed at him, but seemed to relax a little. He went over to the dead man and rolled him over with the toe of his boot. Arnold Mayer stared sightlessly toward the sky. One less crook to trail.

"Ma'am, I'm a U.S. Marshall. I've been hunting this man and two of his partners for weeks." He took a wallet with his badge and identification in it and tried to hand it to her. She glanced at it, but didn't take it. It took two hands to aim the heavy rifle and she wasn't letting her guard down for a minute.

He tried again. "Are the other men here? Are they in the house? I know their horses are in the corral. Why didn't they take their saddles off?"

He never took his eyes off her face. Suddenly she gave a big sigh, shrugged and lowered the gun.

"Let's see your badge."

He handed her the wallet. She took a good look before handing it back. As if a dam broke, she began to talk.

"They came up and threatened me. They wanted me to feed them and let them hide out here. My husband is . . . gone. I went into the bedroom to . . . to . . . and got the gun and shot them while they sat at the table. I don't think they expected me to be able to shoot or be armed at all."

"Wait. You shot all of them? Where are they? What are you doing with Mayer here?"

She turned, took her horse's reins again and began to drag the grisly burden toward a huge boulder that edged the clearing. He followed, leading his horse behind the body. On the far side of the boulder was a shallow grave with two bodies already in it. She led the shying horse beside the grave until the body was close to the opening.

Jack said, "Wait. Let me see who they are. I need some identification if they have any." He carefully stepped into the hole and looked at the dead men. Before he could check for papers, she said, "I took what they had in their pockets. It's up at the house. I'll give it to you when I'm through."

He helped her roll the third man into the hole, took the shovel she had leaning against the boulder and filled in the loose soil. The grave wasn't deep enough to keep predators out, so he carried loose rocks from the slope above and covered the grave site. She helped find rocks though he could tell she was exhausted.

"Who are you?"

"My name is Jack Delancey. Who are you?"

"I'm Lily Reynolds. I thank you for your help. I knew I had to get these bodies underground soon. I wanted them . . . out of sight."

"I understand." He took the reins of her horse and his and let her lead the way back to the cabin. "Why are the horses in the corral saddled?"

"They tied them to the rail. I didn't take time to unsaddle them after I shot the men. I couldn't just turn them loose."

"Let's go inside. We can talk about this after you rest. May I put my horse in your corral now? He's as tired as I am."

She must have realized how weary she was. She blinked as she considered his request. She could hardly turn him away after all his help.

"That's fine. There's hay for him. I'll . . . be inside."

Jack led both horses to the barn, unsaddled his, rubbed him down a bit and forked some hay into a manger. He didn't turn him out into the corral with the other horses. He might need to catch him quickly. He hoped not. He unclipped the bridle from her horse and put a halter on it. As he turned to the hay mow, he stumbled over a saddle thrown down in the middle of the barn. Automatically he picked it up and positioned it over the gate to a stall. Who would throw a saddle down like that? He took an armload of hay to the corral. The saddled horses came to the treat. He grabbed their trailing reins as they bent to eat and relieved them of their saddles and bridles. No rubdown for these beasts.

He staggered wearily as he walked to the cabin carrying his bedroll and pack. His quest was over at last. What an unexpected way for it to end. What should he do now? As he stepped up on the porch he knew for sure he had to rest before he made any decisions. He dropped the bedroll and pack on the porch.

Lily had made a pot of coffee and put a loaf of bread and a jar of preserves on a counter beside the stove. She was sitting in a rocker with her back to him when he knocked gently and entered. He gasped as she stood and faced him. She held a tiny baby in her arms. Her look dared him to comment.

"Careful where you walk or sit. I didn't take time to clean up the mess. I doubt that blood will come up easy in any case. There's bread and jelly there. Help yourself if you're hungry." She felt with one hand for the rocker and lowered herself in it. She put the baby on her shoulder and gently patted its back.

Jack stood in the doorway, hat and rifle in hand, trying to take all this in. He eased over to the stove and poured himself a cup of coffee. He cut a slice from the loaf, found a spoon in a holder in the middle of the table and put a little jam on the bread. Leaning against the counter he ate hungrily. Lily took the baby into the other room. He moved so he could see where she went. A cradle was beside the bed and she was rocking it a little to ease the tiny baby back to sleep.

"Ma'am, I'll help you clean up after awhile. Why don't you rest now? That blood is as dry as it's likely to get."

Lily stared at him, gave him a tiny smile and lay back on the bed. "Good idea. I couldn't scrub now if my life depended on it." She was asleep before he could answer.

The blood on the table disgusted him. He found a scrubbing rag and quickly removed all he could from the table top. He would deal with the floor later. He sat down at the table with his cup of coffee in his hand. His head drooped lower, rested on his arm and he slept.

ft

It was long after dark when the whimpering baby woke Lily and Jack. He sat up and tried to figure where he was. She felt her way from the bedroom and lit a lamp. She went back for the baby and again sat in the rocker and fed it. She frowned at him. "Never seen anyone nurse an infant?"

"Not since my wife nursed our son. Sorry if I offend you." He stood and found the wood box, added a few sticks to the stove and pushed the coffeepot onto an eye. His gaze kept returning to the little figure humming to her baby.

"Tell me again how you managed to shoot three men. Weren't they armed?"

"Of course they were armed. I guess they were too surprised to shoot back. By the time they figured out where the shots were coming from they were dead. I'm a good shot." Now the words just tumbled out. "I thought about just wounding them, but then what? I could scarcely herd them to town, carrying my baby. They made it plain what they had in mind for me. I knew my child would die and I would, too. I saw the extra horse they brought with them."

"What do you mean? Is there another horse around here loose?"

"No. We only have the one saddle horse. I was using her to drag the bodies. I reckon they met my husband somewhere along the trail to town." With a strangled sob she said, "I don't expect him to come back."

Jack stared at her. So it was her husband he had buried. No papers on him, no horse in sight, a single gunshot wound to the back. She read his face like he had spoken.

"You found him, didn't you? Do I need to go bury him now?" She suddenly crumpled up and sobbed. "I dared hope . . . What a fool I am!"

He had never felt so useless.

"I buried him under a big oak off the trail. I'm sorry. I'll take you there if you want. I put a cross to mark the spot and piled rocks like we did for the others."

With tears streaming down her cheeks, she stood, handed him the baby and began to assemble a meal. He was amazed. He hadn't held a baby in years, but old skills weren't forgotten. He looked down into a beautiful little face framed with wisps of dark hair. The baby gazed back at him and sucked its fist.

"What's his name?"

"Margaret's his name. You don't think a boy would be that pretty, do you?"

He chuckled. "Margaret, you have an extraordinary mother. I hope you grow up knowing she saved your life."

"Jack, why are you here? How long have you been chasing these men?"

"Seems like forever. They were murderers and arsonists. There's a big bounty on their heads. When you can ride, we need to go to town and wire the proper people to collect the money."

"You think I want money for what I did?" She turned to him, rubbing the tears off her cheeks. "You think I'd accept money for killing those monsters?"

Jack looked her straight in the eye.

"You'd be a fool to refuse it. You could hire someone to help you here. I can see how much work you and your husband have put into this place. The money is yours."

f_t

Jack waited a week before riding with Lily and Margaret to town. In the intervening time, he helped scrub the bloodstains off the floor, shot a few squirrels for meals and generally made himself useful. He slept on a pallet in the barn. The week gave him time to come to some painful decisions. His quest was over. He could go on with his life.

"What do you want to do with the crooks' horses, Lily? They're yours, I guess."

"Do you think I might sell them? I don't need three more horses eating me out of house and home."

"Sure, let's try to sell them. We can lead them to town when we go next week."

"Then what?"

He played dumb. "What do you mean?"

"What am I supposed to do after next week? You know I can't keep this place going by myself. I lay awake nights wondering what I'm going to do. Joe and I have no family back East. I'm sure you have family to get back to. And your job. Where will you go next?"

"Is Margaret asleep? Let's sit out here on the porch and I'll tell you a story."

They sat on the edge of the porch, legs dangling, eyes on the hills in the distance.

"I was after those men as part of my job, but I took the job for a different reason. You see, Lily, they killed my wife and child and set my house on fire while I was away for the day. I came home to smoking rubble. Neighbors had seen the smoke. They named the men responsible. I went to the Marshall's office in Denver and took a job on the understanding I would try to track these men down first. They'd left a wide swath of misery on their way, so following them wasn't all that hard. I was just hours from them when I came here. You did my job for me. I'm sorry you had to kill three men, yet I'm pleased they're gone." He looked down at his hands. "I had no intention of arresting them."

Lily sat listening, shivering a little at the implications of his words. So that was why he was comfortable with a baby, why he was so handy around her farm.

She said, "We can go to town soon. I'll decide what to do before I get there."

ft

They made a strange sight as they rode down the dusty street. Townspeople stopped in their tracks and gaped. He rode in front, carrying a baby, leading a saddled horse. She rode behind, leading two more saddled horses. The entourage stopped in front of the Sheriff's Office and tied all the horses to the rail. He handed her the baby and together they went in.

The sheriff said, "Your papers look real, Mr. Delancey. These other papers are for three wanted men. Tell me where you got them."

It took an hour to get the story told. The sheriff was skeptical at first.

"I talked to your husband when he was in town over a week ago. You say he's dead? Did this man kill him?"

They took him through the story again. He just sat and shook his head. Jack stood finally and said he had some telegrams to send. He handed the baby to Lily and went to the railway station. When he returned he found Lily just exiting the Sheriff's Office.

"Did you find the telegraph office?"

"Sure. Now what?"

"Let's go eat and I'll feed Margaret. The sheriff finally believed I killed those men. I'm surprised he didn't arrest me for murder."

"Now, calm down. The sheriff will probably send a few wires himself and check out my credentials. He had wanted posters on his wall for all three men. When he settles down I'll go talk to him again. In the meantime, I'm going to put the horses in the livery stable and tell anyone who'll listen that they're for sale with all their tack. I should hear about the rewards by tomorrow. The papers you took off the men identify them, so that should be no problem. By day after tomorrow you can go back home, knowing you have a nest egg in the bank."

"What will you do, Jack? Will we ever see you again?"

"First I'll find someone who'll help you keep your place going. Then I'll go back and settle my estate—what there's left of it. I should be back here in less than a year. If you haven't had any better offers, I'll talk you into marrying me and we'll raise Margaret together. How does that sound?"

Lily raised a tearful face to meet his eyes. "That sounds like a long time to wait, but it would be best, I guess. God go with you, Jack. Come back to me. Our grieving time will be over by then and we can make a good life together."

–The End–

From The Editor

Aren't stories wonderful? To be able, for a while, to travel back in time, to go to the far corners of the country, or even the world. To live great adventures, meet fantastic people, see historic events unfold right in front of your eyes? All that, and more, comes from the mind of a storyteller. My first storyteller was my grandmother. She introduced me to the wonderful world of words, words used to paint pictures in my mind. More vivid than reality, her tales allowed me to go out and fight villains and ride monsters. Heady stuff!

Grand as that was, in a way I'm even luckier now. The stories I get are written. Instead of traveling miles to my grandmother's house, then waiting for her to have time to sit down and regale me with her latest twist on "When Grandpa Shot the Whale," now, wherever I am, I can pick up a book or eReader and dive in. So many books, with so many wonderful stories in them.

Readers are lucky. We get to experience things most people only dream of. From now on, whenever you want, you can pick up this book and take a trip back to the old West, where justice was more than just the law, and a person's word was his bond.

I am very grateful to all the Western writers who submit their lovingly-crafted stories, and to every reader who visits each month and votes for his or her favorite Tale. Without all of you, FrontierTales.com would not exist.

So keep on writing, reading and voting. Tell your friends about us, and maybe buy a paperback or eBook collection of the "Best of" now and then. They're available from Pen-L Publishing (www.Pen-L.com), Amazon, Barnes and Noble, or can be ordered through your favorite bookseller.

Thanks, and happy trails to you!

Duke

Frontier Tales Ezine

The ezine Frontier Tales was born out of frustration. Back in 2009, I couldn't find anywhere to send my Western short stories. Dusty Richards, who had over 150 published Western novels under his belt, happened to live in the same area of northwest Arkansas that I do, so I asked him. Dusty told me there was much uncertainty facing authors because of the changes in the publishing industry. Book stores were going out of business and magazines were almost a thing of the past. Those were scary times for writers.

I was just a beginner at this fiction-writing business, but I knew what we needed. I decided to create an online magazine devoted to Western short stories, and Frontier Tales was born.

A lot of stories have now seen the light of day and a lot of writers, new authors as well as veterans, have gotten exposure they wouldn't have otherwise found. We've published hundreds of stories now, and more are coming out each month.

I never did see one of my stories in print (or ebook) but I take pride in helping other authors achieve the goal of getting published. And one of these days I hope to join them!

Frontier Tales has received a wonderful reception and reaches viewers from around the world, with readership almost doubling every year. If you're a writer, whether a greenhorn or old hand, consider sending us your polished Western frontier story. (See guidelines at **www.FrontierTales.com/Submissions.php**)

The Best of Frontier Tales Anthology, Volumes 1, 2, and 3 featured the stories from the first three years that were voted Favorite of the Month. Now, here's the fourth year's Best. I hope you enjoy them!

Duke Pennell

Be sure to peruse the rest of the Frontier Tales Best-Of anthologies at

www.Pen-L.com/BoFTA.php

−|−

And sign up for monthly notices when
new issues of the ezine come out:
www.FrontierTales.com

Read—Vote—Tell a Friend—It's FREE!

If you like, please Like our Facebook page at
www.facebook.com/FrontierTalesEzine

−|−

Did you enjoy this book?

If you did, we'd love to hear about it.

Please leave a review with Amazon, Goodreads, or Barnes and Noble.

Thanks for supporting your Western authors!

More great books at
www.Pen-L.com
Books You'll Love!